THE MYSTERY OF THE DRAMATURGICAL DAGGER

THE THREE INVESTIGATORS

IN

THE MYSTERY OF THE DRAMATURGICAL DAGGER

BY

ELIZABETH ARTHUR
& STEVEN BAUER

BASED ON CHARACTERS
CREATED BY ROBERT ARTHUR

Hollow Tree Press 2025

CONTENTS

1

A Letter From Daman Duwalia

Bob Andrews glanced at his watch. His lesson on the climbing wall in the Rocky Beach High School gym was over, and soon he'd be on his way to the Jones Salvage Yard and a meeting with his best friends and Three Investigators colleagues Jupiter Jones and Pete Crenshaw. Today they were going to be discussing the possibilities for their next investigation, and he wanted to be on time.

Although Bob and his friends wouldn't officially enter high school for another six weeks or so, they'd already been asked to sign up for a sport for their freshman year, and Bob had picked climbing. This wasn't just because he had a good frame for it, but because, a few years before, he'd broken his leg in multiple places while climbing alone, and he didn't want that experience to make him afraid of climbing in the future.

Even so, he'd decided that roped climbing, with a partner, was probably a good idea. Bob took off his helmet and stared up at the wall. It sure didn't look like real rock. In fact, it looked just like what it was – a highly engineered irregular vertical surface – mottled brown and gray, made of fiberglass, resin, and metal, covered with ridges, bumps, and indentations, places to grab or to put your toe. It offended Bob in some obscure way – did it have to be so ugly? – and was certainly nothing that anyone would mistake for the real thing.

"Great first lesson," Coach Fogerty said. "Come on over to the locker and I'll issue you equipment for the summer."

"O.K., Coach," Bob said. He stood coiling a sturdy nylon rope, one end of which had been attached to a harness he wore. The rope had been looped through an anchor high up near the ceiling, and Coach Fogerty had held the other end. Bob had just learned this was called being "on belay" – a way to prevent a climber from falling and getting injured. He'd only gotten twenty feet off the ground this time, but he'd felt good.

"Did that harness fit you O.K.?" Coach Fogerty asked.

"Yes, sir," Bob said.

"Not too tight? Not too slack?"

Bob grinned. The coach sounded as if he'd just read Goldilocks.

"It was just right, Coach," Bob said.

"Good," Coach Fogerty said. He rummaged in the locker. "Now here's a chalk bag for keeping your fingers and hands dry; you've already got the rope and helmet. And here's a bag of anchors and chocks. And a second harness."

"Thanks," Bob said. "And thanks for your help."

Rocky Beach High had an outstanding summer athletic program for all students, including recent graduates and those who'd be students in the fall, and Bob had thought it would be good to get a head start.

"My pleasure," Coach Fogerty said. "Good to meet you. Always glad to find a new climber. Have you got a climbing partner?"

"I don't know yet," Bob said. "Maybe. She's just moved to Rocky Beach from Scotland, but she used to climb there with her father. Right now, she's working for Jupiter's aunt and uncle at the Jones Salvage Yard. She's going to be a freshman at Rocky Beach High this fall, too."

When Bob had first gotten to the gym and met Coach Fogerty this morning, he'd told him a bit about Pete and Jupiter and their work as The Three Investigators. Coach Fogerty hadn't read any articles about their exploits,

but he *had* seen the Salvage Yard – like everyone else in Rocky Beach. With its seven-foot-
high wooden fence painted with colorful histori-
cal murals running completely around the
Yard, and a set of filigreed wrought-iron gates
guarding the entrance, it was a hard place to
miss. Although he and Pete and Jupiter actually
had missed it so far this summer – using "miss"
in a different sense, of course! Their first three
cases had all taken them to central California,
and they'd agreed that it would nice if their
next one let them stay at home.

"I look forward to meeting her," Coach
Fogerty said, smiling. "She sounds interesting."

Bob thanked the coach again, then
headed for the locker room. He suspected he
knew why the Coach had smiled, but unfortunately, although Bob *was* hoping he could persuade Mallory to go climbing with him – and
not just because he needed a climbing partner
for roped climbing but because he had a crush
on her – he didn't think the feeling was mutual.

In the locker room, Bob showered,
changed into his street clothes, and grabbed his
backpack. Although he was heading to the Salvage Yard and he normally brought his laptop
to his meetings with Pete and Jupiter, today
he'd left it home. There was nothing in his

backpack but a book his mother had just lent him – *Darwin's Moral Mammals* – and a manilla folder containing a bunch of e-mails he'd received in his role as Records and Research for The Three Investigators.

He'd held this position from the time he, Pete, and Jupiter had formed their firm, and he'd always enjoyed it – he was good at it, and his friends had always appreciated his work. However, six weeks before, when The Three Investigators' friend, mentor, and chronicler, the mystery writer Hector Sebastian, had moved to Wyoming, Bob had suddenly found himself not merely supplying case notes to a more experienced writer, but writing the reports from start to finish himself.

At the beginning of the summer, The Three Investigators had finally established a website. Bob had been posting the reports online, but although he'd worked hard on them, and Pete and Jupiter and his parents had all told him they were terrific, so far he'd been disappointed at how few other people seemed to have read them – especially because Bob had come up with what he considered the great idea of giving his case reports titles in alphabetical order.

Still, after their first case that summer, in

which they'd uncovered a cache of hidden gold, two or three people had written in wanting help with finding gold, and after their second case, in which the discovery of a forged letter had resulted in the unmasking of the villain, there had been several e-mails about possible document forgeries. The latest batch of e-mails was focused on counterfeit money, Bob thought with some amusement.

But while none of the inquiries had seemed likely to lead to an interesting new case, today he and his friends would weigh the options and decide which one had the most potential. He pulled his manilla folder and *Darwin's Moral Mammals* out of his backpack and stuffed his climbing gear in, then put the folder and the book on top.

He hadn't had time to crack the book, but Bob's mother was an evolutionary biologist who taught at Reedmore College, and she'd thought he might be interested in its thesis. She'd told him the book argued that moral behavior was hard-wired into human beings because evolution had made cooperation with other people desirable. She'd also said it looked at specific human emotions in order to show that, although each of them could do damage in excess, there were good reasons why each had evolved in the first place. Although he didn't have a scientific bone in his body, these ideas made sense to Bob.

Just then, the cellphone in his pocket rang loudly. He opened it to see the words "Three Investigators Headquarters." Jupiter was calling from the landline in the Salvage Yard.

"Jupe?" he said after he punched the button.

"Good morning, Records," Jupiter said. "Ramble and scramble."

"Wow!" Bob said. *Ramble and scramble* meant Bob should get to Headquarters – a banged-up mobile home trailer in the Jones Salvage Yard – as soon as he possibly could. Jupiter hadn't used the code in a while – he thought it was too juvenile, now – and besides, Bob would be arriving in almost no time anyway.

"What's up?" Bob asked.

"We've got a case. And you're going to like it," Jupiter said. "I don't know what kinds of inquiries you have in your manilla folder, but if you're still at home, you can leave it there. We won't be needing it. Someone pretty famous is interested in our services. And he's right here in Rocky Beach. For the summer, anyway. Or until he draws his last breath."

"Well, tell me! Who is he?" Bob asked.

"I can't," said Jupiter. "I promised Pete I'd let *him* tell you when you got here. But I thought I'd better warn you that Pete's about to bust a gut. He seems to feel that this is the most exciting thing that's happened in Rocky Beach since tall ships docked in its harbor."

"Can't you even give me a hint?" Bob said.

"I already have. Several, in fact," Jupiter said. "Just get here as soon as you can."

"I will," Bob said. "I'm at the high school, though. I just had my first climbing lesson. Is Mallory working today?"

"Yes," said Jupiter. "But this is no time to try to persuade her to go climbing with you at Palisade Point. We have more important things to do."

"I'll be right there," said Bob.

He punched his cellphone again and put it in his pocket, cinched his backpack tight, then shrugged it onto his shoulders. As he pedaled toward the Salvage Yard, he thought about what Jupiter had said. That someone pretty famous was interested in The Three Investigators' services – and that he was right here in Rocky Beach.

"For the summer, anyway," Jupiter had said. "Or until he draws his last breath."

Now, what on earth had *that* meant? Although Bob was hardly as good at puzzles as Jupiter was, he'd had some real successes at solving them in the past, and it would be great if he could figure out who this famous person was while on his way to join his friends. Was some famous person dying? And why was this person, whoever he was, only in Rocky Beach for the summer?

Or maybe that was the wrong way to tackle the problem. Maybe Bob should just consider the kind of person that Pete would be really excited about having the chance to work for. Oh, well, it was too late now, Bob thought, as he caught sight of Green Gate One, biked past it, then turned into the Salvage Yard. Yes, Mallory was here, Bob confirmed, as he saw her bicycle parked by the front office. It meant she was working, and maybe later he'd have the chance to see her.

In the meantime, he found Pete and Jupiter waiting for him in the outdoor workshop, and the minute he saw them, he realized he was a bit disappointed that he wasn't going to have a chance to show them the inquiries he'd gotten in response to his case reports. One of these days it would be nice if they got a case solely because of his efforts to publicize their firm.

It was a hot and sunny day, and Jupiter sat in a green metal chair reading a book with stars and moons and suns on its cover, while Pete was kicking a small, round bag filled with sand into the air. When he saw Bob pull in, he kicked the bag high and caught it with his hand.

"Have you guessed who it is yet?" he called out excitedly as Bob brought his bike to a stop and jumped off. "He's just here for the summer! But I saw him once on the set of a movie my father worked on!"

"An actor?" asked Bob, surprised.

"A *movie* actor!" said Pete. "But this summer he's playing Romeo at the Rocky Beach Summer Theatre Festival!"

Although Pete seemed to feel that that was all Bob would need for him to guess who Pete was talking about, he had absolutely no idea.

Still, the reference to Romeo at least clarified for Bob that when Jupiter had said that Mr. Whoever-He-Was was in Rocky Beach for the summer, or until he drew his last breath, he had probably been referring to the fact that in William Shakespeare's play *Romeo and Juliet,* Romeo died every night on stage.

Bob hoped that Mr. Whoever-He-Was wasn't afraid he was going to die for real.

"Well, I still don't know who he is," Bob said, a little plaintively. "What movie did your father work on that he was in?"

"That was Jupe's clue!" Pete crowed. "When he said I thought this was the most exciting thing that's happened in Rocky Beach since tall ships docked in its harbor! It was the movie about the 18th-century British Navy. You remember! I think we talked about it sometime after we found out that one of Worthington's grandfathers had been a Lascar!"

By now, Bob was feeling seriously hot and bothered. What did Worthington's grandfather have to do with the guy who was playing Romeo? And anyway, wasn't the star of that movie some Indian actor named Raj Khan? As far as Bob could remember, Raj Khan must have been about fifty years old, and Romeo was supposed to be quite young.

"Just tell me," he said through gritted teeth.

"It's Daman Duwalia! The star of the *Time Twist* series!" Pete said triumphantly. "And guess what? Although he wrote a real letter to Jupiter, instead of sending an e-mail to you or our website, in his letter he said that he was impressed not only with the way we solved our cases, but with the way you wrote about them!"

All of a sudden, Bob's tension dissolved and he started grinning from ear to ear.

"Not really?" he said.

"Really," said Jupiter. "That's why Pete wanted us to tell you in person." He pulled a fancy-looking envelope out from underneath his book, extracted a letter from it, and handed the letter to Bob. "We've both read it twice, so there's no need to read it aloud. Just read it to yourself."

Bob sat down next to Jupiter, took the letter, unfolded it, and stared at it for a moment before he started reading.

Daman Duwalia! he thought. Though Bob hadn't seen any of the *Time Twist* films, he knew that Duwalia was already a star — a young Indian actor whose parents had worked in Bollywood before immigrating to California, where Daman had been born. He'd started acting himself at an early age, doing the usual goofy comedies when he was too young to do anything better, but then he'd been cast in a movie that had made him famous, and since the movie had had two sequels, he was now very famous indeed.

Still, this summer he was working at the Rocky Beach Summer Theatre Festival – a very old festival, well-known throughout the area for casting a mixture of professional actors and local talent, and whose building had recently undergone an extensive renovation.

His letter said that the Rocky Beach production of *Romeo and Juliet* was, coincidentally, being directed by a woman named Madhuri Singh – also of Indian parentage, but born in London – and that both he and she had received threatening anonymous letters. The letters had been typed on a typewriter, not printed by a computer. In addition, both she and Daman had had what he called "really strange experiences" – he in his dressing room, she in her office. And Madhuri Singh had also had a number of odd, though minor, accidents.

That was really how it had all started – when Daman Duwalia had noticed that Madhuri Singh had started coming to work injured, one day with her ankle bandaged, another with a Band-Aid on her face. When Daman had asked, she'd told him she'd cut her face on a prop rapier that had been purposely left sticking straight out from a wall, and she'd sprained her ankle when she'd tripped over a box of props she was sure hadn't been there five minutes earlier.

Still, if it hadn't been for the threatening letters, he explained, neither of them would have thought anything about the accidents, and even *with* the letters, neither one of them wanted to call the police. There really *was* such a thing as the wrong kind of publicity, he wrote. Even though *Romeo and Juliet* didn't have a curse on it, the way Shakespeare's play *Macbeth* supposedly did, if word got out that weird things were happening on the production, it might be bad for the box office.

Since he'd been feeling a little freaked out, Daman Duwalia had gotten online and looked up private detective agencies in Rocky Beach. His search had brought him to The Three Investigators, and although he hadn't understood just how *young* Jupiter, Pete, and Bob were at first, he'd been truly impressed with Bob's case reports. After he'd read them, he'd talked to the girl who was playing Juliet – a local girl named Califia García-Williams – and she'd told him that she'd long been in the same grade at school as Jupiter, Pete, and Bob.

Since Califia was just fourteen, this had

surprised Duwalia, he said, but when Califia had told him how mature The Three Investigators were for their age, he'd decided they might be able to get to the bottom of what was going on at the theater. Madhuri Singh seemed to think he and she were being targeted because they were Hindus, but Daman Duwalia found that hard to believe. If they could make it, he hoped The Three Investigators would meet him at the theater the next day at noon. The actors had a two-hour break for lunch, and unless he heard they couldn't come, he'd expect to meet them at the box office, then take them to his dressing room to talk.

Bob finished reading the letter and looked up at his friends.

"Wow!" he said. "The idea that someone as famous as Daman Duwalia would come to us for help is just – amazing."

"And you're the one who brought him to us, Records," said Jupiter.

"Did you notice he gave us his cellphone number?" Pete said. "I bet I could start a business selling that to the girls in our class! Though Califia wouldn't need it."

Califia García-Williams had been in Jupiter, Pete, and Bob's grade for a long time now, but Bob didn't know her very well. Mallory MacLeod had recently told Bob that Califia's mother was a dancer and her father was an actor, but before he'd learned this, all Bob had really known about her was that she was very pretty and was in the dance and theater clubs.

Like Bob, she had mixed parentage – his was Scottish/Chinese and hers was Hispanic/African-American – but unlike Bob, she had a lot of acting talent.

"I take it we're going to meet Duwalia?" he asked – mainly for the pleasure of listening to Pete erupt with a gigantic "Are you kidding me?"

Actually, Pete didn't stop there but began reviewing several high points of the first *Time Twist* movie and was starting on some high points from the sequel when Jupiter held his hand up.

"Enough," he said. "You've convinced me that Daman Duwalia is talented. The mere fact that he was cast as Romeo in a summer theater production of Shakespeare's tragedy wouldn't guarantee that, unfortunately. The director might have simply wanted a famous name as a box office draw."

"*Romeo and Juliet* is a tragedy?" Pete asked in surprise. "I thought the Rocky Beach

Summer Theatre Festival put on mostly feel-good stuff, if you know what I mean."

"*Romeo and Juliet* definitely isn't feel-good," Bob said. "It takes place during the Renaissance in Verona, Italy, and although it's a love story, a lot of people die."

Although Bob had never seen a live production of any Shakespeare play, he'd seen film versions of *Romeo and Julie*t and *Hamlet* – both by the Italian director Franco Zefferelli. He'd liked *Hamlet* better, but he'd thought the actors playing Romeo and Juliet had been really effective at conveying how desperately they wanted to be together.

"Verona?" Pete exclaimed, delighted. "Verona has great soccer teams. They call it football in Italy, but still. I thought you said it was a love story!"

"It is," Jupiter said. "A tragic love story. I've never seen it, but I'm pretty sure there isn't any soccer."

"In that you would be correct," Bob said, smiling. "There's a lot of sword fighting, but no soccer. Romeo's family and Juliet's family hate each other, but Romeo and Juliet secretly get married. It's a tragedy because they die in the end."

"I hate it when that happens," Pete said.

"The Greek philosopher Aristotle thought watching a tragedy made the audience feel emotions like pity and terror," Bob said. "And that led to a healing experience he called *catharsis*."

When this didn't seem all that enlightening to Pete, Bob added, "It's like when you cry a lot, and then when it's over you feel better."

"In any case," Jupiter interrupted firmly, "if we're going to be meeting Daman Duwalia at the Rocky Beach Summer Theatre Festival tomorrow at noon, we should go into Headquarters and use the firm computer to do some preliminary research."

"Oh, no," Pete groaned. "It's really hot in there today. I'd much rather stay outside for now. Maybe Bob can boot up his laptop."

"I didn't bring it," Bob said. "I only had room for the climbing gear. Anyway, I think the first thing we should do is call Worthington and make sure he can drive us to the theater tomorrow."

The Rocky Beach Summer Theatre Festival was in the foothills outside of town, and while, theoretically, the boys could ride their bikes there to meet Daman Duwalia, it was quite some distance – with a lot of it uphill – and it seemed to Bob they shouldn't arrive disheveled, sweaty, and out of breath for such an important meeting.

It would be years before the three of them were able to get their driver's licenses in California, but a few weeks ago, they'd bought a used car with part of the reward money they'd gotten after discovering a pouch of gold hidden for over a hundred years. The reward had also let them hire Worthington – who they'd met when he had driven them around in a Rolls-Royce Jupiter had won the use of, and who'd become a real friend.

"Good thinking, Bob," Jupiter said. "Do you have your cellphone with you?"

Since he *did* have *that*, Bob dialed Worthington's number – but was sent right to voice mail. He left a brief message saying that he, Jupiter, and Pete were hoping Worthington could drive them somewhere the following day, then clicked his phone shut.

"We really need to do some research about Daman Duwalia, Madhuri Singh, and the Summer Theatre Festival," Jupiter said. "The only personal knowledge I have of any of those relates to the new building. The architect's plans called for lots of recycled materials, and the construction crew bought reclaimed lumber from the Salvage Yard. Aunt Mathilda was quite beside herself."

"I remember!" Pete said. "She was practically dancing with joy."

"I helped out when the crew came to the Yard," Jupiter said, "so I met some of the men working on the renovation. I particularly remember a man named Cory Johnson. He was on the electrical crew and was buying old light fixtures he could use in the restrooms, dressing rooms, and halls. He was going to rebuild most of them. He seemed very clever – a natural inventor."

"Like you," Bob said.

"Well," Jupiter admitted. "I did feel a certain kinship."

"That's so cool!" Pete said. "When we go to the theater, maybe we'll recognize stuff."

"In any case, unless the two of you have something to add, we should go in now," Jupiter said. "It's too bad Bob doesn't have his laptop, but since no one else around here has one either – "

"Mallory does!" Bob found himself saying. "She uses one in her work at the Salvage Yard. It's hers, but she always has it. At least she's had it every time I've seen her working here."

"That's a great idea!" Pete exclaimed,

though Jupiter looked somewhat doubtful.

"Also, she and Califia are getting to be friends," Bob added. "Before we headed up to Cornucopia Wines for the Fourth of July, Mallory told me that Califia had invited her to go swimming at her house. Maybe Califia has even told her what's going on up at the theater."

"I can't believe Califia is playing Juliet," Pete said. "I always thought she was really talented, but I didn't know she was good enough to play opposite someone like Daman Duwalia!"

"Don't you remember when we were in sixth grade and Miss Thomas organized that assembly where students memorized poems?" Bob asked. "Everyone started applauding when Califia was done reciting."

"That's right!" Pete said. "I do remember."

For a moment, Jupiter still looked uncertain about the proposal, but then he nodded and said, "Fine. Go and find Mallory. I'll go to the house to get us all some drinks."

Pete and Bob both jumped to their feet – Pete to start kicking his hacky sack into the air again, and Bob to head for the shed he thought Mallory must be working in – while Jupiter started toward the gate at the back of the Salvage Yard.

As he walked toward the shed, Bob was glad that Jupe had agreed about Mallory. Of course, Bob knew that what had sealed the deal hadn't been Mallory's laptop – or even the help she had given The Three Investigators in two of their last three cases – but the fact that she was a friend of Califia's and might know more than Daman Duwalia had told them in his letter.

Even so, Bob was pretty sure that, although Jupiter had spent most of his life thinking girls weren't just a different sex but a different species, his mind was slowly being changed – and mostly thanks to Mallory MacLeod. Like Jupiter, Mallory had a lot of self-confidence, and decisions seemed to come easily to her. She also seemed to have a Jupiter-like drive toward finishing things and getting results.

Bob liked these qualities in Mallory partly because he had also seen them in Jupiter – though of course, with Mallory, it was all slightly different. And, to Bob, intriguing. As he walked up the steps into the shed where he thought he'd find her working, he stopped when he saw her through the open door. A laptop was open in front of her and there were piles of colorful scatter rugs to her left and to her right.

She was sitting cross-legged on the splintery wooden floor, wearing old-fashioned loose-fitting blue jeans and a peasanty-looking coral-colored blouse with sleeves that came down just to her elbows. Her hair was wavy and very red – a kind of red that almost knocked your eyes out, Bob thought. Although at this distance he couldn't really see her eyes, he knew they were very blue, and that there was something about those eyes and that hair that really got to him.

However, the most amazing thing about the situation was that the girl herself was easy to talk to, and when she looked up and saw him, he found himself calling out.

"Hey, Mallory," he said. "Do you want to help us research a new case? We've been hired by Daman Duwalia! Well, not hired, exactly, but he's asked us to meet with him tomorrow! And he wrote to us because he read my case reports on our website!"

2

A Shakespearian Curse

Ten minutes later, Mallory found herself in The Three Investigators' outdoor workshop. To her left was an old printing press − the kind where you had to hand-set the letters − and to her right were three or four serious-looking metalworking tools. Mallory had never sat down in the workshop before, and she was flattered that Bob, Pete, and Jupiter had invited her to join them there.

"So this is where you take non-working things your uncle finds and turn them into working things?" she asked.

"Not always. Just sometimes," Pete said.

"Most of the stuff I'm cataloguing isn't working or non-working," Mallory said. "It's just stuff."

When Mathilda Jones had hired her to work in the Salvage Yard, she'd told Mallory to set her own hours, and before Mallory had left the shed, she'd signed out for the day − and without any regret, even though her new job was almost always interesting and exciting.

This was partly because she liked old

stuff and partly because Aunt Mathilda had given her both responsibility and freedom. No doubt she trusted Mallory to work unsupervised because she and Jupiter's uncle had lived with Jupiter for a lot of years now, and had gotten used to the idea of trusting young people.

Even so, when Bob had shown up in the doorway of the shed and invited her (and her laptop!) to join The Three Investigators, she'd been delighted to do it. Ever since she'd helped Jupiter, Pete, and Bob find a pouch of hidden gold, she'd been more and more interested in what they did in their investigations, and more and more eager to get involved with them.

Of course, she knew she couldn't say this – or even act too enthusiastic – but from the moment she had met him, Jupiter Jones had reminded her, just a little, of her own father. Her father had been an engineer and an inventor who had total faith in his ability to come up with solutions to even the most difficult problems. He'd liked thinking outside the box and, in his own way, so did Jupiter.

Jupiter had lived with his father's half-brother Titus and Titus's wife Mathilda in a house behind the Salvage Yard ever since his parents had died in a car accident when he was an infant – although on a recent case that had taken them out of town, he had unexpectedly discovered some previously unknown relatives of his mother's.

Jupiter hadn't talked about this much since it had happened, but Mallory could tell that it had made him feel a little differently about himself. Now that he knew his mother and father had both been astronomers, Jupiter was reading books about the universe. As well, he hadn't seemed as eager as usual to move from one case directly to the next − though that seemed to have changed today, Mallory thought.

"So," Pete said, clapping his hands decisively. "Did you love *Time Twist*, or did you love *Time Twist*?"

"Haven't seen it," Mallory said.

Pete looked amazed. "What?" he said.

"I haven't seen it, either," said Bob − and soon Bob and Pete were telling her about the letter Daman Duwalia had written to The Three Investigators, and their appointment to meet with him the following day.

Mallory had recently talked with her new friend Califia about what had been going on at the Rocky Beach Summer Theatre Festival; in fact, just a few days before, Califia had invited Mallory to visit her there. She'd introduced her to Daman Duwalia, and before she plunged into online research, Mallory thought she might mention a few things that Califia had told her. She'd been drinking a soda Pete had given her, but when Jupiter asked if she'd be willing to get online to find out everything she could about the Rocky Beach Summer Theatre Festival, she set the soda down.

"Sure," she said. "But I'm guessing that Daman didn't say in his letter that his parents had played Romeo and Juliet in a Bollywood film version of the story."

At this, Jupiter looked interested, as Mallory had hoped he would.

"No," Jupiter said. "He didn't. In fact, I had no idea that Bollywood ever made films based on Shakespeare. For Daman Duwalia's parents to have starred as the ill-fated lovers seems a curious fact."

"I thought you might think it was relevant," Mallory said. "As it turns out, Califia has a sort of crush on Daman, and the two of them have been talking about their lives."

"What else has Duwalia told Califia?" Bob asked her.

"Has he talked about the *Time Twist* movies?" Pete said excitedly.

"I don't think so," Mallory said, smiling.

She found she was liking Pete more and more – and not just because he made her laugh. In fact, although Mallory never got crushes on anyone – just on words and ideas and writers and books and places – if she had, she might have gotten a crush on Pete. His enthusiasm was contagious, and he seemed to really like other people. If he'd been a girl, she would have said he was vivacious. As it was, she'd call him exuberant – and in a way that was both authentic and attractive. Plus, he was very good-looking.

Of course, because she and Bob were both bookish, Bob was easier for her to talk to than Pete was – though what she liked about Bob was a little harder to put into words. She liked how devoted and loyal he was to his friends, but she also liked how dedicated he was to getting things *right*. She had the impression that when he undertook a task, he would complete it if he possibly could.

Also, he'd been the driving force behind a gift The Three Investigators had given her in thanks for her work on the pouch of gold case – the gift of a beautiful handmade reproduction immigrant's trunk painted with her name and the year of her arrival in the United States. She'd found this incredibly touching, and she loved it every time she saw it sitting underneath her bedroom window.

However, in the case of The Three Investigators, what she was *really* getting to like was the three of them together under Jupiter's leadership. Jupiter was − well, in a way, he was a conundrum, a puzzle, and an enigma, but in another way he was gifted with what might be called strategic intelligence. He had a big picture view of the cosmos which, to Mallory, was almost irresistible. What was attractive wasn't Jupiter himself, of course, but his conviction that, with the proper combination of analysis and tactics, every goal could be achieved.

"Anyway," Mallory went on, "Daman told Califia that Indian audiences are almost obsessed with *Romeo and Juliet*. In the last seven years, Bollywood has made at least seven versions. They've all done incredibly well − but for the strangest reason. The story is about a love-match in the face of family opposition, and in India love-matches are a radical concept."

"What?" Pete exclaimed. "How can love be a radical concept?"

"I don't think love itself is," said Mallory. "But in India a lot of people get married not because they love each other but because their parents arrange it."

"I can see why that would make *Romeo and Juliet* a better match for Hindi cinema than, say, *Hamlet* or *Macbeth*," Bob said. "And you know, that reminds me. In his letter Duwalia said the production itself couldn't be cursed, because *Romeo and Juliet* didn't have a curse on it, the way *Macbeth* supposedly does."

"I noticed that, too," Pete said. "What kind of curse, do you think?"

He looked a little nervous as he said this – almost as if he really believed in curses, Mallory thought – and when Bob and Jupiter both smiled, she guessed he probably almost did.

"Well," she said, "you have to understand that *Macbeth* has witches in it."

"Witches!" Pete said.

"Chanting around a cauldron," Mallory said. "You haven't heard of the curse on *Macbeth*? If you'd grown up in Scotland, you would have."

"I don't really know what it is, either," Bob said. "All I know is that actors call *Macbeth* 'the Scottish play,' because they think that speaking its real name aloud in a theater causes bad luck."

"If I'm remembering right," Mallory said, "legend has it that the play's very first performance was struck with disaster. In school we were told that either the actor playing Lady Macbeth died suddenly and Shakespeare had to play the part himself, or that a real dagger was accidentally used in place of a stage dagger for the murder of King Duncan, and the actor playing him really died."

Since that was all she could remember, Mallory grabbed her laptop and typed in the search terms "curse," "Macbeth," and "Scottish play" – which led her, in very short order, to further information.

"The story about the real dagger seems to be the most famous," she said. "But this article on the Royal Shakespeare Company's website says that a lot of later productions have also had accidents – 'including actors falling off the stage, mysterious deaths, and even narrow misses by falling stage weights,'" she read. "It also says that supposedly a real coven of witches was upset that Shakespeare used actual chants, so they cursed the play itself."

"Yikes!" said Pete. "I had no idea you could curse a play!"

"You can't," said Jupiter mildly. "But since there are always hazards to any enterprise in life, and since actors and actresses tend to have vivid imaginations, it isn't really surprising that legends about *Macbeth* have developed over time. However, Daman Duwalia isn't in *Macbeth*. He's in *Romeo and Juliet*, and the most interesting thing I've heard so far is that *Romeo and Juliet* has a special attraction for Indian audiences. Can you tell us more about that, Mallory?"

"I can try," she said. When she'd discovered a relevant article in the *Spectator*, she skimmed it. She looked up when she was finished.

"It says that in traditional Indian culture, parents believed they knew best for their children, and felt that choosing someone from a good family was better than leaving the whole thing up to chance," she reported. "They wanted someone with a strong education who was from the right class. But things are changing, and a lot of Bollywood films are now making fun of arranged marriages, and showing people in love."

Just then, Mallory heard the sound of a car turning into the gates of the Salvage Yard, and although the outdoor workshop was partially screened, when she looked up, she saw a blue and white mini-Cooper drive in and park.

"It's Worthington!" Bob exclaimed.

The four of them jumped to their feet and headed for the Mini-Cooper from which

Worthington was unfolding his long frame in what seemed to Mallory a kind of magic trick. Mallory had only recently met Worthington, but she liked him a lot. He'd been very considerate of her – linking the two of them by calling them both "ex-pats," driving her and the immigrant's trunk The Three Investigators had given her back to her apartment, and – most memorably – rousting her hated cousin Skinny Norris when he'd been lounging outside her front door in his sports car.

"So tell me," Pete asked Worthington. "Are you psychic?"

Worthington laughed. "I happened to check my phone when I wasn't far from here, so I decided it would be just as easy and more enjoyable to stop in."

He looked up and caught Mallory's eye. "Hello, Mallory," he said. "It's a pleasure to see you again – and with no Skinny Norris anywhere about!"

"Hi, Worthington," she said. "Thank you again for getting rid of him so neatly."

"How does the work go," Worthington asked, "cataloguing the wonders of this astonishing place?"

Just then Jupiter's Aunt Mathilda stuck her head out of one of the windows in the Salvage Yard's office.

"Land sakes!" she said. "A body can hardly think amid all this racket. What a lot of noise you boys can make!"

Then she looked directly at Worthington. "Hello, William," she said. "What were you just saying about the wonders of this place?"

Worthington laughed. "Hello, Mathilda. Ears like an owl."

"Yes, indeed," Aunt Mathilda said. "Well, go ahead, Mallory. Answer the man. Tell him how you're doing."

"Very well, thank you," she said. "Of course, we're only in the early stages of uncovering all the great stuff – "

"Great stuff!" Aunt Mathilda said. "You heard the girl!"

"I have no doubt," Worthington said. "I've always thought the Salvage Yard the repository of the greatest stuff. Still, I'm delighted to hear it. And how would you say Ms. MacLeod is doing, Mathilda?"

Aunt Mathilda smiled broadly. "She's doing splendidly, thank you. When the new website is finally ready, I just know we're going to make a lot of online sales. And all because Mallory has sorted and catalogued and described. Couldn't do without her!"

Mallory was happy to hear this public vote of confidence, and particularly pleased to see how impressed Bob and Pete and – yes, even Jupiter – were.

"Well, I'd better get back to work," Aunt Mathilda said. "Time and tide wait for no woman. Now, if the five of you wouldn't mind taking your business just a little bit further – ." She made a suggestive shooing motion with her hands, and then shut the Salvage Yard's office window.

The five of them moved past the Mini-Cooper to continue their talk.

"You said in your message you wanted me to drive you somewhere tomorrow," Worthington said to Bob

"Yes," Bob said. "We need to go up to the Rocky Beach Summer Theatre Festival. We're supposed to be there by noon and stay for a couple of hours."

"A new case?" Worthington asked.

"We think so," Jupiter told him. "They're mounting a production of *Romeo and Juliet*, and some strange things seem to be happening. We'll know better after we meet with our prospective client."

"And who might that be?" Worthington

asked.

"Guess!" Pete said. "No! Let me tell you!" He paused for dramatic effect. "Daman Duwalia!" he said. "From *Time Twist*! Isn't that amazing? Have you seen any of those movies, Worthington?"

"I haven't had the pleasure," Worthington said. "But I'm aware that Daman Duwalia has made quite a success of himself since I knew him. We played opposite each other in one of his earliest movies."

"No way!" Pete said. "You know Daman Duwalia?"

"Yes, indeed I do," Worthington said. "Though I haven't seen him in some time. This was about seven years ago now. Young Duwalia was just ten. I was cast, as almost always, as an English chauffeur. I was assigned to drive an obnoxious rich child around town while his parents were otherwise engaged. I took him shopping at a department store with his father's credit card. We fed the sea lions at the zoo. That sort of thing."

"Was it fun?" Pete asked.

"Driving The Three Investigators is fun," Worthington said. "This was strictly work, though I did take a shine to young Duwalia. After all, he wasn't to blame for the treacly plot."

"What *was* the plot?" Bob asked.

"You can imagine," Worthington said. "Absent self-absorbed parents whose child acts out through his egregious behavior. The obliging servant becomes a father figure to the child master. It was supposed to be a comedy, but it wasn't funny. Still, young Duwalia was very professional. Always on time and never complaining. He was very self-possessed for a ten-year-old. And of course, since he and I both have Indian forebears, there was a fellow feeling as well."

"I find," Jupiter said, "that I am developing an unexpected sympathy for Da-man Duwalia."

"Why is that?" Mallory asked. Both Pete and Bob had laughed when Jupiter said this, but she wasn't in on the joke.

Bob hastened to explain. "Jupiter's aunt got him involved in acting for a while when he was very young," he said.

"A very short while," Jupiter said, "and I am still in the process of forgiving her."

Mallory laughed. She liked Jupiter's dry wit more and more.

"Do you know anything about the Rocky Beach Summer Theatre Festival, Worthington?" Jupiter added.

"Not a great deal," Worthington said. "Other than the fact that the new artistic director is Sir Iain Anthony. There was quite a lot of media attention paid when he was appointed two years ago."

"You mean the famous English actor?" Mallory asked.

"Yes," Worthington said. "He played all the great Shakespearean roles. And then, as so many fine British actors do, he also found work in Hollywood. He retired five years ago, after he was diagnosed with Parkinson's disease."

"Gee," Pete said. "That's too bad."

"But when the artistic directorship opened at the theater," Worthington said, "he was selected for the position. He was a natural, of course. Nothing helps raise money like star power, and the theater was just about to begin fundraising for its renovation. It was a coup for Rocky Beach when Sir Iain said yes."

"Do you know him personally?" Jupiter asked.

"I wouldn't say I know him," Worthington said. "Everyone calls him Sir Iain. But I have met him once or twice. Somewhat imposing but very gracious. And of course he has that wonderful rich voice. I imagine you boys will meet him yourselves if you're going to be investigating a mystery at the theater."

"Wow!" Pete said. "That would be fantastic."

"But you don't even know who he is!" Bob said. "I mean you didn't until Worthington told us."

"But he's famous, isn't he? Well, not as famous as Daman Duwalia."

"I think he's a good deal more famous," Worthington said smiling. "At least, in certain circles."

"And besides," Jupiter said. "We have to remember that fame is a fleeting thing, and not worth much in the end."

"Oddly enough, Shakespeare would probably agree with that. Again and again in his plays, he reveals how dangerous the desire for fame can be," Worthington said.

"Will you be able to pick us up at 11:45 tomorrow morning?" Jupiter asked. "You can say hello to Daman Duwalia when we get there."

"I'd like that," Worthington said. "But I won't be able to stay at the theater while you're meeting with him. I've got another appointment. I'll have to come back to get you later on."

He suddenly turned to Mallory. "And you? Will you be coming, too?" he asked.

Since Mallory felt quite certain, without even looking to see, that Jupiter wouldn't want her to say yes, she kept her eyes on Worthington.

"I'm sure The Three Investigators can handle their appointment without my help," she said, very firmly. "But my friend who's playing Juliet has invited me to come see her and Daman rehearse the tomb scene tomorrow afternoon, and I'm supposed to bicycle up at about 2:00."

She turned to the boys and added, "I'm sure Califia wouldn't mind if you stayed on and watched the rehearsal with me. It might shed some light on whatever you learn at your meeting."

"That actually would be better for me," Worthington said. "It would have been tricky for me to get back to pick you up by 2:00, but if you stay an extra couple of hours, it will be no problem. We can load Mallory's bike on the Flex, and bring her back with us."

"That would be brilliant," Mallory said. "If the boys can do it," she added.

"I don't see why not," said Jupiter.

Mallory was pleased to hear him say

that. It seemed that her plan not to push him too hard was beginning to work.

Worthington said goodbye, and after he drove away in his Mini-Cooper, Mallory turned to Pete. "Now remember. When you get to the theater tomorrow," she said, "the play is *Romeo and Juliet*, not *Macbeth*. Nothing to be superstitious about."

"I don't know about that," said Pete. "Maybe that coven of witches decided to curse a few of Shakespeare's other plays!"

Mallory was sure Pete didn't really think that but had said it partly to prove he'd been paying attention when she'd been talking, and partly to make her smile. Superstitious or not, he was a sweetheart, Mallory thought.

Still, even with Pete, it would be wise to be careful. After all, The Three Investigators had known one another for a long time now – ever since they'd met in kindergarten – and even more than she liked the boys individually, she liked them as a *unit*. She didn't want to disturb the truly impressive functioning of that unit – which was strong and resourceful and resilient and a lot of other admirable things.

3

Magnetic Attraction

The following morning, Pete and his friends were sitting on the raised wooden porch of the Salvage Yard's office, waiting for Worthington. Jupiter was reading his book on astronomy while Bob was doing research on his laptop. But Pete felt restless, sitting and doing nothing except thinking.

Even after years of knowing Jupe and Bob, it still seemed to him that thinking wasn't really *doing* something. At least, when *he* was the one who was thinking. Jupiter was a great thinker, and Bob was a good one, but he himself had only a limited capacity to ponder anything before he wanted to jump to his feet and *go* somewhere. He really liked that aspect of their cases, so he'd really liked this summer; already he and Bob and Jupiter had been to Sonoma and Auburn and Jackson – places pretty far away from Rocky Beach.

They'd also bought a car, and met Mallory MacLeod. It was cool having a girl operative, Pete thought. Of course, he knew that Bob would make fun of him if he actually used that phrase aloud, but since he was just *thinking*, there could be no harm in it. After all, he had used the phrase for years before Mallory turned up – and to be honest, even now, she wasn't actually a girl operative at all.

Still, she might be, someday, and in the meantime, it was fun to have her around. Pete was a bit worried that Bob might like her more than he and Jupiter did – that he might actually *like* her, so to speak – but Bob was very sensible, and very loyal, and even if he *did* like her in that way, he wouldn't let it affect the way he worked as one of The Three Investigators. Or at least Pete hoped he wouldn't. The three of them had been tight for a long, long time now, and Pete wanted it to stay that way.

Luckily, before Pete had time to think too much more, Worthington drove into the Salvage Yard in his Mini-Cooper, climbed out, headed for the Ford Flex, and climbed into the driver's seat. Ever since Worthington had started driving them in their own car, Pete had been riding shotgun, and he greeted Worthington enthusiastically and was soon fastening his seat belt.

"This is great!" Pete said as Worthington started driving toward the theater. "Being driven to a famous theater run by a famous actor to meet another famous actor by a guy who was once in a movie with that actor!"

"That guy presumably being me, Master Crenshaw?" said Worthington, smiling.

Pete blushed very easily, and he found himself blushing now as he struggled to think how he could have phrased his thought a little better.

"I'm sorry, Worthington," he said. "I didn't mean that *you* aren't famous, too! To us, you definitely are!"

"There's only one Worthington," Bob agreed, from the back seat.

"I actually *did* want to be famous once," said Worthington. "But now I'm glad it never happened. Ambition can be a two-edged blade – a good thing if it makes you want to grow in knowledge and expertise but a bad thing if it makes you push everything else in your life aside. In Shakespeare's *Henry V* a boy being urged to go into battle says, 'I would give all my fame for a pot of ale and safety,' and most normal people would agree with him."

"Do you think the desire for fame is abnormal, then?" asked Jupiter.

"Not at all," said Worthington. "I shouldn't have used the word 'normal.' A sense of purpose is not only normal but vital if you want to live a happy life. When I first arrived in Hollywood, I took classical acting lessons, and fencing lessons, and falconry lessons, just to see how far my talent would take me. It didn't take me very far, unfortunately, but I've never regretted being serious about it when I was young."

"You took *fencing*?" Pete asked, impressed.

"I studied with a very well-known teacher at the Center for Falconry and Fencing," Worthington said. "If he were still alive, he might be choreographing the fight scenes in the Festival's production of *Romeo and Juliet*."

Pete remembered that Bob had said there was sword fighting in the play, but until Worthington referred to it, it hadn't occurred to him that Daman Duwalia would probably be doing some of the fighting. He could hardly wait to see that, he thought, as Worthington started to ascend the final hill that led to the Rocky Beach Summer Theatre Festival's home. He turned into the driveway and parked in front of the newly renovated building.

Pete and Bob and Jupiter – and probably Califia – had all been brought here on a field trip when they were in 4th or 5th grade, but Pete hadn't been here since, and all he remembered was that the building the theater was housed in had originally been an old horse barn – a huge central barn with a lean-to on either side. In those days, the building had actually looked as if someone might still keep horses in it, Pete thought.

Now, however, it was totally different. At the front was a new entrance with glass doors leading into a lobby, the lean-tos on the sides had been changed into fully constructed wings with windows, and at the back there was a second addition Pete assumed must contain offices and dressing rooms and stuff like that.

The exterior was clad in wooden clapboards which had been cut so that each one had a wavy pattern, and they had been put on horizontally in some places and vertically in others. Skylights had been added to the addition at the rear, and – except for the skylights – all of the doors and windows seemed to have wooden frames, not metal ones.

"Wow," said Bob in what sounded like genuine awe. "This is a really impressive job. The stone patios are beautiful, and so is the building. That wood and those windows didn't come from the Salvage Yard, though – there's just too much of both of them."

"I agree," said Jupiter. "I'd guess that

the architect stipulated that the recycled lumber from the Salvage Yard be used inside, along with the recycled light fixtures. Outside, the materials seem to be brand new."

"Can you believe how great this is?" said Pete. "Whoever the architect was, he – or she – should be famous!"

"It's an excellent job," Jupiter agreed. "Done by someone who took the job very seriously."

"The box office must be in this lobby at the front," Bob said. "That's where Daman Duwalia told us to meet him."

Jupiter glanced at his watch. "We're a little early," he said. "That side door is standing open. Let's see if it takes us into the main part of the theater. If the actors are in rehearsal, we can watch them. Worthington, you should come with us so that you can say hello to Daman Duwalia when we do find him."

"Yes, indeed," Worthington said. Pete went first, up a winding path that brought them to a series of granite steps leading to the opened door on the right-hand side of the building.

Inside, he was amazed to see that what had once been merely a lean-to had been turned into an elongated reception room – an area with comfortable sofas and easy chairs with tables, with an exit door at the back, and at the front, a bar and a refreshment center.

There, a woman with a bandana over her hair was getting lemonade from a dispenser. She was wearing white harem pants that ballooned around her legs and a red shirt with a sequined vest, and even from the back she looked vaguely familiar to Pete. When she heard footsteps, she turned and looked at them with dawning, pleased surprise. Pete saw that it was Charlotte Mitchell, who the boys had met at Isabella Chang's when she'd invited them to dinner to celebrate the successful conclusion of her case.

By now, Bob and Jupiter had also recognized Charlotte, and almost simultaneously the three of them exclaimed, "Charlotte! What are *you* doing here?"

She laughed, picked up her lemonade, and walked toward them.

"Howdy, you three!" she said. "I could ask you the same question, except I'm sure that whenever you're together, you're on the track of some mystery or other. I'm here because I'm the props manager for *Romeo and Juliet*. I've always loved the theater, but I'm terrible at acting, so eight years ago I started volunteering on the stage crew."

By this time, she was looking inquisitively at Worthington, so Jupiter introduced them and told her who he and Pete and Bob were there to see. Charlotte suggested that Worthington and the boys go into the theater and watch a bit of the rehearsal while they waited for Daman Duwalia.

"The lemonade is actually for Sir Iain," she explained. "Sir Iain Anthony. He's the artistic director of the theater, and I work for him part-time, just the way I work for Isabella Chang. In her case, it's because of her eyesight, and in his case, it's his Parkinson's, but they're both energetic and amazing people. Well, it's great to see you. Maybe I'll see you again later. And don't forget that if you ever want to visit Isabella, you should call me. I know Bob has my number."

She waved and took off briskly for the door at the rear of the reception area, while Pete and the others moved past the elaborately carved wooden posts that separated the side reception area from the central theater. They soon found themselves at the bottom level of five or six gently sloping tiers of seats, looking at the nearby stage where two men holding swords were dueling with one another while another man stood nearby.

The four of them slipped into seats and watched attentively as one of the men swung at the other and lunged forward; his partner took a few steps back, parried the blow, and then, pointing the tip of his sword, advanced very rapidly. Back and forth they went. Pete was fascinated. It was a lot like dancing, he thought – but dancing with deadly weapons.

Since Worthington was sitting between Pete on one side of him and Jupe and Bob to the other, he was able to whisper to all of them. "This is the fight between Tybalt and Mercutio. In the play, they'll be surrounded by hooting hooligans, but right now they're just practicing the choreography. It's Italian-style fencing. It's mesmerizing, isn't it? Whoever these actors are, they've had some proper training."

"So you know how to do this?" Jupiter asked.

"To some degree," said Worthington. "Although it's harder than it looks."

"I wouldn't say that," Pete said. "It looks pretty hard." Then all of a sudden the rehearsal was over, the actors were leaving the stage, and Jupiter was saying, reflectively, "It's a very intellectual sport."

"An argument made visible," Worthington agreed. "I think you might be good at it, Jupiter. If you like, I could give you a lesson or two. Or you could take some instruction at the Center for Falconry and Fencing. I still know a few people there."

Jupiter looked both grateful and embarrassed, but before he had time to respond to Worthington's invitation, Daman Duwalia suddenly appeared next to one of the carved wooden posts dividing the theater from the reception area. There was no mistaking him, even at this distance. He was very handsome, with curly black hair that managed to look both insouciant and perfectly in place. His eyes were dark brown and contrasted with his olive skin.

In fact, he was tall and dark and handsome, and as he scanned the theater, he spotted them and called out, "You must be The Three Investigators. I'm sorry I'm late for our appointment. Charlotte Mitchell told me you were here."

The moment he saw him, close-up, in person, Pete understood why Daman Duwalia had become a star. His smile was dazzling, and he radiated charisma. Bumping into one another in their eagerness to be agreeable — and to assure Daman Duwalia they weren't annoyed – Pete and Bob and Jupiter hurried toward where he stood waiting, with Worthington bringing up the rear. Shortly, there were handshakes all around; Pete looked at his hand furtively after Daman Duwalia had held it, then stuck it in his pocket with a sense of awe.

"So you're Bob Andrews?" Daman asked. "The one who writes the blog? You write really well."

Bob stood speechless as Daman looked past him to Worthington. Across his face spread the same pleased and dawning recognition Charlotte Mitchell had shown The Three Investigators.

"You may remember William Worthington playing a chauffeur in one of your early films," Jupiter said. "He's been driving in real life for some years now, and he brought us up to the theater today."

"Mr. Worthington?" said Daman Duwalia. "Is that really you?"

Worthington's voice grew deeper, and his British accent more pronounced. "'Well, young master," he said. "It's time for the two of us to go home. Perhaps your parents will have returned from Borneo. If not, we can watch the peacocks on the lawn.'"

Everyone laughed.

"You didn't really say that, did you?" Pete asked.

Worthington nodded and reverted to his own voice. "It seems *Drive On, Mr. Beasley* was the silly beginning to what's turned into an interesting career," he said. "From balderdash to the Bard in less than seven years."

"Though even the Bard wrote balderdash from time to time," Daman Duwalia said, smiling. "Still, I'm lucky to be in this production. I'm glad *Time Twist* has been a big success, but one more minute of flying through space in what looks like a giant silver thimble and I'd have been stuck playing a single role for the rest of my life."

"Wait a minute," Pete said. "I *love* that thimble!"

Duwalia laughed as he looked at the four of them with pleasure. "Before I tell you what's been happening, would you like me to show you around the theater?" he asked.

"Would we ever!" Pete said.

"It might be useful to understand the layout," Jupiter said.

"I'll leave the four of you alone now," Worthington said. "You'll find that these lads are expert investigators, Daman. You'll be in good hands with them."

To the boys, he said, "I'll be able to get back here any time after 3:00. Just call me on my cellphone when you're ready to get picked up."

After Worthington left by the side door, Jupiter took out his wallet.

"Before we start, I want to give you one of our cards," he said. "I know you've already seen our website, but the card also has the number of our landline in Headquarters and the number of Bob's cellphone at the bottom."

He and Pete had just recently hand-printed a whole new batch, and Pete was proud of the role he'd played in it. The card read

THE THREE INVESTIGATORS
"We Investigate Anything"
???
First Investigator – Jupiter Jones
Second Investigator – Pete Crenshaw
Records and Research – Bob Andrews

and as Daman Duwalia studied it, he looked suitably impressed.

"I'll program these numbers into my cellphone as soon as I get the chance," he said, slipping the card into a pocket. He led the way backstage where he showed The Three Investigators the sets and the catwalks, as well as the elaborate overhead devices for handling the lights and the other necessary equipment for any given play.

"That's called the fly," he explained, pointing overhead. "And that room at the back of the theater is a highly sophisticated control room. When the play is running, there's always someone in it, managing lights and sound and stuff."

The boys walked toward an exit door on the far side of the backstage area. They passed racks of Elizabethan costumes, and then Daman paused before an open doorway.

"This is the prop room," he said, leading the way in. Pete saw that the room had wall racks and boxes filled with gear, mannequins, and tables on which colorful props were displayed. At the back was a second door – presumably leading into the rear addition to the theater. Two of the tables held various objects that Pete knew had to be used in the play – goblets, a jumble of fancy glittery masks, a lute and other stringed instruments – and a third held swords, sword belts, and daggers.

"Wow!" said Pete. "Are these real?"

"Real enough," Daman said. "The edges have been blunted to cut down on the possibility of injury. But you still need to know how to use them."

"Have you ever been hurt in a sword fight?" Bob asked.

"Once or twice," Daman said. "Mostly bruises. One cut on the arm."

He picked up a wicked-looking dagger and pressed its point to his palm. Pete watched, astonished, as he began putting pressure on the blade and the dagger's hilt moved closer and closer to his hand. He almost expected to see the blade come out the other side, but Daman smiled and showed them how the blade retracted into the hilt.

"This is the dagger Juliet uses to kill herself in the play's climactic scene," Daman explained. "From a distance, it looks as if she's really stabbing herself in the heart. Luckily, this one *isn't* real."

Pete was taken by the strangeness of everything – the costumes, the odd smells, the pools of light and shadow, the weapons that weren't really weapons. He was also fascinated by the long thin swords and picked one up. It had a sort of wire basket that spread around his hand, but its blade was slender, double-edged and sharp-pointed – though both the edges and tip had been blunted.

"That's a rapier," Daman said. "In the early Italian Renaissance, swords like that were just coming into use in Verona and also in London. People were afraid they were having a bad influence – encouraging deadly fights in the streets. They certainly do in *Romeo and Juliet*."

Experimentally Pete swept his arm and listened to the whistle the steel made as it cut through the air – at which Jupiter also picked up a rapier and did the same thing. Somehow Jupiter looked a lot more comfortable doing this than Pete felt.

Pete was just about to set the weapon down when a young man came into the room through the same door they had entered. He was dressed in tights and on his belt he wore a sword on one side and a dagger on the other. As he walked into the room, he unbelted them and tossed them on the weapons table.

"More fans, Duwalia?" he said in a nasty tone of voice. He looked to be eighteen or nineteen, and he had a scruff of beard and dirty blond hair. "Why can't you confine your autograph-giving to non-working hours? And keep the rug-rats out of the theater entirely?" He turned on his heel and left the room as rapidly as he'd come into it.

"Rug-rats!" Pete said indignantly. It had been years since anyone had called him that – and even then it had been a joke. Pete felt truly insulted, and although he was anything but violent, he suddenly felt he could understand wanting to take a poke at someone with a rapier. In fact, he took a few steps toward the door, holding the blade aloft and stabbing the air with it.

Jupiter, on the other hand, carefully set the sword he'd been holding back on the table.

"Sorry about that," Daman said, to all of them. "It's the kind of occupational hazard I'm used to, though. What I'm *not* used to is getting anonymous death threats."

"Wasn't that the guy who's playing Tybalt?" Bob asked. "Juliet's brother?"

"That's right," Daman said. "At least I get him in the end. After he accidentally kills my kinsman Mercutio in a mock street fight, I take after him in a rage and kill him. That's what causes all the problems in the play – or most of them."

"Do you think he's the one who sent the letters?" Pete asked. He could easily believe it, after that insult about rug-rats.

"To be honest, I don't think he has the required skill-set," Daman said. He smiled, but

Pete could tell that he wasn't happy about what had just happened – that it had reminded him of why he'd contacted The Three Investigators in the first place. It had also taken the fun out of showing them the prop room.

Pete really felt for Daman, suddenly, and to make him feel better, and lighten the mood again, he lifted the rapier he was holding into the air, took a few steps back as he'd seen the actors do on stage, and then, step by step, holding the blade aloft, he moved forward.

"*You're* the dirty rat!" he said to a mannequin in a corner, stabbing in its direction while the tip of the rapier quivered.

In front of the mannequin was a small table on which a large unsheathed dagger had been set, and although it was some inches below the rapier's blade, as Pete comically parried and thrust, he had the sudden feeling that the rapier had been grabbed by an unseen hand – one strong enough to drag a steel blade downward. The tip of it suddenly dipped, of its own volition, toward the table.

"Yikes!" Pete found himself saying, and then – and without him directing it – the tip of the rapier moved down even further and hit the dagger's blade with an audible click. When he pulled his blade away in a panic, the dagger started to come with it. Instinctively, Pete shook the rapier in order to try to disengage it from the dagger, but he was so alarmed by what was happening that he jerked harder than he had meant to, and when the dagger dropped, it landed on the floor and skidded halfway across the room. As it skidded, it whirled around.

"Watch out!" Pete yelled. "Be careful! I think that dagger's cursed!"

Then he watched as the dagger came to a stop in front of Jupiter – who bent to pick it up.

4

Hollywood, Bollywood, Schmollywood

Until the moment Pete, apparently magically, picked up the dagger on the tip of his rapier and then sent it skidding across the floor, Jupiter hadn't been feeling particularly engaged in this new case.

For one thing, although Daman Duwalia seemed a nice enough guy, Jupiter was unimpressed with fame for its own sake, and – in the absence of further information about the matter – he thought the most probable explanation for the anonymous threatening letters was simply that he *was* famous, and therefore, by definition, envied.

In addition, ever since Jupiter, Pete, and Bob had gotten back from a visit to their new friend Branko Petrovic during which Jupiter had met some brand-new relatives, he'd been thinking about things other than Three Investigators cases. Hearing the dagger clatter as it whirled across the floor changed that.

Of course, on top of the clatter, Jupiter had heard the surprised gasps of Bob and Daman – as well as Pete yelling about the dagger being cursed. Since he knew as well as he knew anything that objects *couldn't* be cursed, before the dagger had even come to rest in front of him, he'd started to formulate a theory about what had happened.

Like any theory, this one needed to be tested, so after Jupiter bent to pick the dagger up, he set it on a table. He was surprised to find that it was very heavy – clearly not a prop weapon, but a deadly-looking knife. The steel was not uniformly shiny but held an intricate and detailed pattern of whorls and curvy lines. He could feel himself beginning to focus.

"This is real," Jupiter said, as Pete set the rapier he'd been holding down on the same table and he and the others crowded around to look at the dagger. From its tip to the end of its grip it was a foot long. It had a wooden handle and a metal guard, and it was double-edged and razor sharp – as Jupiter discovered when he ran the edge of his thumb across the blade. He whistled.

"There's nothing at all blunt about these edges," Jupiter said.

"But why did my rapier stick to it like that?" asked Pete.

"I think I know," Jupiter said. He reached into his pocket, took out his Swiss

Army knife, and opened the largest blade. He touched the steel of his own knife to the steel of the dagger and felt them click together at once.

"As I thought," he said to the others. "The dagger has been magnetized. It's the dagger, not the rapier, that carries the charge."

To prove it, Jupiter reached across the table and touched his Swiss Army knife to the tip of the sword Pete had been holding. Nothing happened, just as he had expected.

"Magnetized!" said Pete.

"But why?" asked Bob. He picked up the dagger and examined it carefully while Jupiter closed the blade of his Swiss Army knife and tucked it back into his pocket.

"That's an interesting pattern," Bob said. "Does that have something to do with the magnetism?"

"I don't think so," Jupiter said. "But what I want to know is how and why the blade got magnetized in the first place. Also, what is a deadly weapon doing here among these stage weapons?" he asked Daman.

Daman looked puzzled but not shocked.

"I've no idea," he said. "I can't remember seeing it here before, and as far as I know, there are no magnets in the theater. There certainly aren't any in the play. But we can add this to the list of strange events I asked you here to talk about."

It was indeed bizarre, Jupiter thought. Although he'd had no trouble guessing that the dagger's odd behavior had been caused by magnetism, it was harder to think of any plausible reason why it might have gotten that way to begin with. So, for the moment, it might be best to focus on other things.

"Yes," said Jupiter. "And we should probably go to your dressing room now so that you can tell me about the others."

Daman nodded and had just turned toward the rear door of the prop room when it opened and a man in his late thirties or early forties entered. He was tall and thin, with a boyish, friendly face. He wore jeans and a yellow t-shirt, and he smiled as he looked at Jupiter – seeming to recognize him at once.

It took Jupiter a little longer to recognize *him*, but then he realized it was Cory Johnson – the man who had come to the Salvage Yard the year before to buy old-fashioned light fixtures for the renovation of the Theatre Festival building.

"Can that be Jupiter Jones?" Cory said. "I'd remember you anywhere."

"Cory Johnson?" Jupiter said. "Are you still with the theater? I thought you were just working on the renovation."

"That was the idea," Cory said. "My degree is in electrical engineering. Though I mostly design electrical systems, I also end up solving problems and testing equipment. They kept me on for the summer to make sure everything goes smoothly. Since I'm good with computers, I'm also working as the computer manager on two of the shows."

He paused and looked around him at the prop room. "Now why did I come in here, exactly? Was I looking for something, or was I lost? Hi, Daman," he said.

"Hi, Cory," said Daman. After Cory nodded at him pleasantly, he took one last look around the room, then turned on his heel and left again. Daman followed him out the door, and Jupiter, Pete and Bob were right behind him.

By now, they were in the new wing of the theater, at the back, and as they walked down a hushed sconce-lit hallway, Jupiter recognized the sconces from the Salvage Yard. In this part of the building there were offices and rehearsal rooms as well as dressing rooms, and shortly Daman was pausing before a wooden door that held an elegant brass nameplate with a card with DAMAN DUWALIA slipped into it. He opened the door and invited The Three Investigators in.

The room had no windows, but it was spacious and well-lit and had a skylight that could be opened and was open now. On top of a bookshelf against the wall, and on other shelves around the room, sat four painted plaster statues, each a foot or more high. The one that first drew Jupiter's attention depicted a seated semi-clad childlike figure with an elephant's head. Its ears were curled forward as if to hear better, its forehead and trunk were richly decorated with markings, and the trunk's tip curled around a basket filled with goods. It looked out at the world with an expression both mild and amused. On its head was an elaborate jeweled crown.

"I see you're interested in Ganesha," Daman said. "He's my favorite Hindu deity, actually — the patron of arts and sciences. He helps in getting rid of obstacles, and he's the god of wisdom and intellect."

"Are you a believing Hindu?" Jupiter asked.

"No," said Daman laughing and shaking his head. "But my director, Madhuri Singh, is.

At least I think she is. Anyway, these were here when I first arrived, along with a bunch of flowers, and a note welcoming me to the theater."

Pete had been standing and staring at the statues. "Do all Hindu gods have four arms?" he asked.

"I don't know," said Daman. "But a lot of them do. These are murtis, though, not gods. Hindus don't worship the murti itself, but the god behind the murti. I'm actually glad these murtis caught your attention, because they're one of the things I wanted to talk to you about."

The boys sat down, and Bob pulled his laptop out of his backpack, opened it, and got ready to take notes. While Bob was setting up a file, Jupiter looked around him – noting the inset lights, the inset sound speakers, and the rich-looking carpeting.

"What do you want me to start with?" Daman asked Jupiter when Bob nodded to indicate that he was ready.

"Why don't we start with Madhuri Singh?" Jupiter said. "In your e-mail, you said you'd both received threatening letters, that you'd also both had strange experiences in your dressing rooms, and that Madhuri Singh had had a series of inexplicable, though minor, accidents."

"Wow!" said Daman, looking at Jupiter admiringly. "That's exactly what I said. I'm amazed you remember it so clearly."

"Jupiter remembers almost everything," Pete said proudly. "But even *I* remember that you said this had started when you noticed that Madhuri Singh was coming to work injured!"

"Yes," said Daman. "At first I thought she must be accident-prone, but when she told me about the box of props and the rapier sticking out of the wall, I wasn't so sure. Of course, those things could still have been total accidents, but the strange experience we both had really couldn't."

"What was yours?" asked Jupiter.

Daman looked at him as if considering how to answer. "Before I tell you, I think I should say that Hinduism is actually quite a complicated religion – one with two radically different kinds of murtis. The ones you see here in my dressing room are called shanta or saumya murtis. They impart a sense of peace and compassion, of kindness and love. When you look at them you feel positive emotions. But there's another kind, called raudra or ugra murtis, and they are totally different. They express anger and even violence. Their eyes are big and round and scary, and instead of fruits and flowers, they carry bones and skulls and weapons."

"Yikes!" Pete said.

"They're supposed to make you feel afraid. And they work," Daman said. "One morning when I came into my dressing room, all these murtis you see were gone. Someone had replaced them with raudra murtis. I'm generally not very superstitious, and I don't easily get creeped out, but when I saw them I wanted to get out of here as fast as I could.

"My stomach clenched and I started shivering, and I found myself running out of the room, and then out of the theater. I went for a walk, did some stretching exercises and took a lot of deep breaths, and when I had calmed down, I came back to find that the dressing room looked just as it does now. All the raudra murtis were gone, along with the creepy feeling, and the shanta murtis were back."

"Holy smokes!" Pete said. "Maybe your dressing room is cursed, too!"

"Pete!" said Jupiter. "What are we going to do with you?"

Pete smiled. "I was only kidding."

"Anyway," Daman went on. "Because Madhuri was the one who put the murtis in my dressing room to begin with, I told her what had happened. And then she said that the exact same thing had happened to her! She came in to her office one morning to find the place crowded with raudra murtis and a feeling of terror, and she got out of there fast. When she went back later, her office had returned to normal. By the way, she asked me not to tell anyone about her experience, so I'm breaking a confidence in mentioning this. I feel badly about that, but I don't see how I can expect you to figure out what's going on if I don't give you all the facts."

"Does this door have a lock on it?" Jupiter asked.

"No," Daman said. "There are so many people in and out of these rooms from month to month, from production to production, that it just wouldn't make sense − too many problems with lost or misplaced keys. So we basically just trust one another."

"That's too bad," Jupiter said. "Not that you trust one another, but that we can't limit our suspects to people with keys. Who knows about the murtis in your dressing room and Madhuri Singh's office?"

"Oh, lots of people," Daman said. "I'm pretty outgoing, and almost everyone in the cast has been in here at one point or another. And the crew."

"Including the guy who plays Tybalt?" Jupiter asked. "It was evident he's jealous of your fame. Maybe he wouldn't mind giving you a scare."

"I guess it's possible," Daman said. "His name is Reginald Ward, and he's some sort of distant relation by marriage to Sir Iain, so I really wouldn't have thought of him as being a suspicious character. And where would he have gotten the ugra murtis? But there's more."

"Go on," Bob said.

"It was only after I told Madhuri what had happened with the murtis that she told me someone had been slipping threatening letters under her office door. The letters had been typed on a typewriter, rather than on a computer."

Jupiter had been waiting for this detail to come up again. Ever since he'd read Daman's initial letter of inquiry, he'd been pondering how best to trace an anonymous letter of this sort.

"It may prove very helpful that your anonymous correspondent used a typewriter," he said. "Before computer printers came along, typed letters varied a lot from one to the next, and sometimes mysteries could be solved simply because a particular piece of writing could be proven to have been typed on a particular machine."

"That's right," Bob agreed. "My father told me that each individual typewriter has its own signature, so to speak."

"So you think you may be able to trace my letters to the machine they were typed on?" Daman asked.

"Theoretically," Jupiter said, "yes. In fact, since there are so few working typewriters still in use, it might even be easier these days than it was when there were a lot of them. After all, anyone still using a typewriter must need to get it serviced and repaired from time to time, and there can't be that many typewriter repair shops still around."

He pondered this for a moment. "However, the first thing we need to do is get more information about the content of the letters. What did Madhuri Singh's letters say? Were they the same from one to the next?"

"No," Daman said. "They were all different. All short and all threatening. All telling her that something horrible was going to happen to her – a fire, a car accident, a cobra in her mailbox. Some mentioned specific Hindu gods, she said. Of course, I never saw her letters myself."

"A cobra!" Pete said

"After I got some threatening letters, too, Madhuri said we must be targets because we were Hindu, but that we couldn't call the police or *Romeo and Juliet* would never see the light of day."

"May I see the letters?" Jupiter asked.

"I've made copies you can take with you," Daman said. He opened a drawer in his dressing table, pulled out three pieces of paper, and handed them to Jupiter.

The first one read:

"Hollywood, Bollywood, Schmollywood. You and your lover parents are doomed to death. Remember the Thuggees?"

while the second one read:

"Is this a dagger I see before me, the handle toward my hand? I think it is, lover baby, and thus with a kiss you die."

and the third one read:

"Yama the great lover is going to get you if you don't watch out."

Jupiter read the letters twice, concentrating both on their content and their form. He was delighted to see that in all three letters, the "a"s and "e"s were floating just above the line while the "l"s were floating just below it; as he had hoped, the typewriter the letters had been typed on had developed idiosyncrasies over time.

"The typewriter *does* have a signature," he said. Then he looked inquiringly at Daman and asked, "Who is Yama?"

"The Hindu god of death," Daman said. "And, of course, the quote about the dagger is from *Macbeth*."

"From *Macbeth*!" Pete exclaimed. "Our friend Mallory MacLeod told us about the curse a coven of witches put on that play! Not that I believe in curses," he added hastily, "but she said that a lot of productions of the play have been struck with disasters – and that an actor was killed for real the first time it was put on."

"That's true," Daman said. "At least it's true that that's the legend – though I was actually more unnerved when I found the raudra murtis in my dressing room than when I found these letters. They really seem pretty stupid – especially the one mixing the quote from *Macbeth* with a quote from *Romeo and Juliet*."

"I noticed that," Bob said. "One of the

most famous lines in *Romeo and Juliet* comes when Romeo says 'And thus with a kiss I die.' But Romeo doesn't die because of a dagger, he dies because he takes poison."

Jupiter thought about this last remark. Since he knew little about Shakespeare's plays, he couldn't really judge the contents of the quote, but it did seem curious to him that someone had mixed up quotes from two different plays. He was also struck by the fact that although the first letter and the last one were specifically Indian in their references, the second one was not.

As Jupiter knew from his reading, the Thuggees had been a cult of Indian assassins – a loosely organized gang of men who robbed and murdered for a living. They would dress in traveler's clothing, join a group of travelers, strangle one or more of them with a knotted silk garrote, then take the murdered person's goods.

Although Jupiter didn't know if Daman knew all the grisly details, he assumed that just as Daman knew that Yama was the Hindu god of death, he must, at least, know that the Thuggees had been Indian assassins. For that reason, the first and third letters seemed to have been written by someone specifically targeting a Hindu. The second letter was different. It could have gone to any actor – or any human being – and its message would have been fully understood.

Jupiter also found the repetition of "lover" from one letter to the next one a curious detail.

However, before he had time to get into a discussion of any of this, he and the others were startled to hear a fire alarm go off. Bob quickly closed his laptop and thrust it into his backpack, while Jupiter clutched the copies of Daman Duwalia's letters as they all jumped to their feet and ran into the passage. There, the alarm was even louder – although soon interrupted by a cool female voice saying, "Please exit the theater in an orderly manner. Please exit the theater in an orderly manner."

What orderly would be under these circumstances, Jupiter wasn't quite certain, but he took the time to examine a chart on the wall where the fire exit routes were clearly marked. Soon he, Bob, Pete, and Daman were standing outside the theater on the side they had come in. There, they found people talking quite calmly about what had happened. Apparently the alarm had been triggered by a fire in Sir Iain Anthony's private office.

Sir Iain had been smoking his pipe and had carelessly tapped its ashes into his wastepaper basket, then left the building – at least according to the excited chatter. The ashes had smoldered, then ignited some paper.

Luckily, Madhuri Singh had been walking by when it happened, and she had pulled the fire alarm in the hallway, then rushed into the office and put the fire out herself. There was no real damage done – except, perhaps, to the wastepaper basket.

"I heard Madhuri say that, since Sir Iain has Parkinson's, you really can't blame him when things like this happen," one of the actors said.

"You can if he burns the theater down!" another one said. "I'm amazed he's allowed to smoke inside his office."

"Someone told me he might not have Parkinson's at all," said a third one. "That it might be some sort of dementia. I can't remember the name, but it has the word 'body' in it somewhere. It's supposed to cause paranoia and hallucinations and irrational rage and stuff like that."

"Maybe *we* should be the paranoid ones!" the second actor exclaimed.

Another bell went off – this time sounding the All Clear – and the actors headed back into the building, leaving Daman and the boys behind.

Still holding his copy of the threatening letters, Jupiter turned to Daman. "Did you hear what those actors were saying? Have you heard anything similar?" he asked.

Daman smiled ruefully. "Ever since rehearsals started. I can't understand it, though," he said. "I've only met Sir Iain three or four times, but although his hands are shaky, he's never acted strangely. Of course, I don't really know him, but I like what I've seen of him. Even though he was knighted by the Queen of England, he's totally down-to-earth, and still as excited as a kid about the theater."

Just at that moment, Jupiter and the others turned to see an older man approaching. He was tall and slender, in his mid-to-late-60s, with an unruly shock of silver hair, vivid blue eyes, and what seemed a faint and perpetual smile. He had a face of real character and an air of kindly gravity. Daman looked a little worried at the possibility that the man – who was clearly Sir Iain Anthony – had overheard what he was saying, but he just flashed Daman a smile.

"I understand an alarm went off while I

was out of my office?" he asked.

His voice, Jupiter thought, was mellifluous – deep, and rich, with complex and haunting tones.

"I think it's been taken care of, sir," Daman said.

"I'm glad to hear it," said Sir Iain. "Are these boys young actors, too?"

"Just visitors, sir," Jupiter said. "I'm Jupiter Jones and this is Pete Crenshaw and Bob Andrews. We all live in Rocky Beach."

Normally, under these circumstances, he would have reached into his pocket for a Three Investigators card and explained what the three of them did, but since Sir Iain had just become a suspect of sorts in the current investigation, Jupiter thought he had better not. In any case, Daman had contacted them expecting confidentiality.

"I'm pleased to meet you," Sir Iain said, extending a faintly trembling hand to each boy in turn. His grip was warm and friendly. "Welcome to the theater. You must be friends of Daman's. He's a fine young man, and he's going to be a fine Shakespearian actor. I, too, started off with Romeo, but I didn't have the innocence to play the role as it really should be played. I was born to play villains, actually."

"Why is that, sir?" Bob asked curiously.

"Because I understood quite young that villains are just ordinary human beings, and that a villain's actions always seem reasonable to *him*. That's why I loved playing Shakespeare and reading Agatha Christie. They both understood that human character is always on a spectrum – that there are almost no horribly bad guys or amazingly good ones. Just a range of everything in between. Except for Iago, of course!"

Since Jupiter had recently been thinking something similar – though not about Iago, since he didn't know who that was – he was struck by the probable truth of this observation, and he looked at Sir Iain with new regard. It was easy to fall into the trap of thinking that everyone you liked was good, while everyone you disliked was bad, but that was not the reality of life.

"Well, I'd better check in with my handlers," Sir Iain added, smiling. "It was nice to meet the three of you. I hope we'll see you at a performance soon."

"I hope so, too," said Jupiter.

"Absolutely," said Bob.

"You bet!" Pete said.

Sir Iain said goodbye and walked carefully up the granite steps into the reception area of the theater while the boys stood staring after him.

"I see what you mean," Jupiter said to Daman. "It's hard to believe he has anything wrong with the parts of his brain that relate to memory or analysis or decision-making. He's an impressive man. I wonder how the rumors got started."

"That's what theaters are like," Daman said. "Hotbeds of rumor and intrigue. Well, I've got to get ready for rehearsal now." He started to walk away, but then turned and called back over his shoulder. "Did I give you anything you can work with?"

"Absolutely," Jupiter said. And he meant it. Ever since he'd first read about typewriter signatures, he'd wanted to solve a mystery by matching a signature with a machine, and at the moment, doing that match-up looked like the simplest way to discover who was writing the anonymous letters to Daman Duwalia and Madhuri Singh.

In fact, Jupiter was already eager to get back to the Salvage Yard and poke around in the shed where the old machines were stored to see if he could find a typewriter that had keys in the same font and font size as the letters on the pages. He'd already decided that the machine would have to be either a manual or an electric typewriter – one with keys on bars, not a ball that spun around. With a ball that spun around, there would be no way you would end up with letters that rode above or below the line.

The question of how the dagger in the prop room had gotten magnetized might be a little harder to get to the bottom of, but since it would seem to have nothing to do with the case at hand, Jupiter thought he could safely ignore it – although if Mallory MacLeod really showed up to watch the coming rehearsal, maybe he should ask her to examine it. He had seen a similar sort of dagger in her apartment when he and the others had been there in the case that involved the fake Kit Carson letter.

Just as he thought this, a sudden scraping sound in the gravel caught his ear and he looked up to see Mallory MacLeod. She jumped off her bike, wheeled it around, and thrust it into a nearby bike rack

5

An Unusual Number of Suspects

Bob also saw Mallory jump off her bike, but unlike Jupiter, he wasn't surprised at her arrival. He'd been watching her approach ever since her bike appeared at the bottom of the hill. He'd first seen it when they'd been talking to Sir Iain, but by the time she arrived at the theater, there was no one left outside except for him, Pete, and Jupe. Bob smiled and waved at Mallory. She was flushed and a little out-of-breath after the long uphill ride, but she smiled and waved back, then bent over for a moment, her hands on her hips, breathing hard.

"Wow, that's quite a hill," she said, as she straightened up. "Hi, Pete. Hi, Jupiter," she added. "Have you guys seen Califia?"

"Not yet," Bob said.

"We've been consulting with Daman Duwalia the whole time," Pete said excitedly. "You just missed him. He went to get ready for rehearsal."

"Califia already introduced us," Mallory said casually. "He seemed very mature for seventeen."

Although Bob couldn't disagree with that, for a moment he felt a sting of something he thought might be jealousy. Since he'd spent several hours the night before reading *Darwin's Moral Mammals*, he'd recently had this emotion brought to his attention in quite a scientific manner. The book his mother had lent him was a work of popular science – nothing she would have used in a course at Reedmore – but there was something about it Bob found appealing.

For one thing, it didn't just argue that moral behavior was hard-wired into human beings because evolution had made cooperation with other people desirable; it also looked at specific human emotions in order to show that, although each of them could do damage in excess, there were good reasons why each had evolved in the first place.

Of course, not everyone felt all of them, but apparently jealousy was a universal trait – and not just among human beings, but among other mammals, too. Dogs, for example, could be very jealous if another dog was given attention they thought should go to them.

But while the emotion might be both understandable and universal, since Bob couldn't remember having felt it before, he was able to see that in the current situation it was really pretty stupid. He had no reason to think that Mallory liked Daman Duwalia any more than she liked him or Pete or Jupiter.

"That's true," Bob said. "Daman Duwalia seems almost like an adult. It'll be interesting to see him act on stage." He was about to propose that the four of them go into the theater when Jupiter started to talk to Mallory.

"Before we go into the rehearsal," he said, "I'd like to show you a dagger in the prop room. It's a real dagger, not a prop one, and I'm hoping you can tell me where it was made and what it is."

Bob knew that weaponry was one of Mallory's interests, so he wasn't surprised by Jupiter's request.

"I'll try," Mallory said. "Though we need to get to the rehearsal pretty soon."

Jupiter nodded and led the way into the upper side door, then down the hall past Daman's dressing room. He opened the rear door to the prop room, and the first thing Bob saw was Califia García-Williams bending over the table with the prop weapons on it, her short curly hair in a halo around her head.

When Califia heard the door open behind her, she turned. "Mallory!" she said, clearly quite pleased. "You made it! I wasn't sure you were going to get here in time. And The Three Investigators too! Have you come to see Daman about the weird stuff that's been happening?"

"We've already seen him," Bob said. "Jupiter wanted to bring Mallory to look at a dagger that's somehow gotten magnetized."

Jupiter looked around and spotted it where he'd left it – on the table in the corner by the mannequin – and as he went to get it, he said to Mallory and Califia, "It's really sharp, so be careful if you touch it."

"The dagger is *magnetized?*" Mallory said. "How on earth did that happen?"

When Jupiter set the dagger down again – this time on one of the big tables – the two girls crowded around him. Mallory picked it up and examined it.

"It's a beauty," she said. "And it's certainly no prop. It's a Scottish dirk, with a blade made from Damascus steel. I think its handle is made of rosewood. Its guard is also steel, but the pommel seems to be brass."

"Is a dirk different from a dagger?" Califia asked.

"Not really," Mallory said. "A dirk is just a dagger traditionally carried by Scottish Highlanders. It tends to be a little shorter than other daggers, but all daggers have a sharp tip and two sharp edges. They're stabbing weapons. Highlanders also used to swear oaths on their dirks."

With the tip of the weapon she was holding, she pointed to the prop daggers on the table.

"Those are called parrying daggers," she said. "They were used during the 16th and 17th centuries, when duelers often carried two double-edged blades – a rapier in their right hand and a parrying dagger in the left. The dagger was used to parry the opponent's rapier and then sometimes to deliver the *coup de grace* in close fighting."

"That's the way the fight master has choreographed the sword fights!" Califia said. "So is the magnetized dagger old?"

"No," said Mallory. "I'd say it's brand new. It's a reproduction, but a good one. They're doing high-quality work these days. I bet that blade is very strong. It could probably be dropped or thrown great distances, and the blade wouldn't break or chip."

Bob had known that Mallory knew something about weapons, but he was still impressed by this flood of information.

"You said the blade is made of Damascus steel?" he asked. "What's that?"

"Actually, it isn't Damascus steel, exactly. Real Damascus steel was made only in the Middle Ages. Now they make steel that looks like Damascus steel, but isn't. It's also sometimes called Damascene steel, and either way the name refers to the wavy patterning – which looks like damask fabric."

"Damask?" said Califia. "I know what *that* is, at least. I'm wearing a damask dress in the scene where Juliet and Romeo kiss for the first time!"

"I thought 'damascene' referred to a one-eighty-degree reversal in someone's attitude. A conversion," Bob said.

"It does," Mallory said. "A double-edged adjective to match a double-edged dagger."

"Shakespeare loved puns and double meanings," Bob said. "I wonder what he'd do with a damascene dagger."

"Well," Mallory said. "Maybe the dagger could undergo a sudden conversion and decide not to stab anyone."

"Or maybe it could just go from being magnetic to nonmagnetic," Califia suggested.

Although Jupiter looked mildly amused at this conversation, he was clearly gearing up to interrupt it when the door to the prop room opened again and a woman with intense brown eyes walked in. She had light brown skin, black hair cut just above her shoulders and attractively disarranged around her face, small hoop earrings and a diamond stud in her left nostril. She was in her late thirties or early forties and moved with an easy grace and authority. She was smiling as she walked toward them.

"Oh, there it is!" she said. "I've been looking for that everywhere. Is the sheath here as well?" She scanned the weapons table, found a leather sheath, and slipped the dagger in it. "What a relief!" she added. "I was getting worried." Bob heard just a trace of a British accent.

She turned to Mallory and the boys in a friendly and open way.

"Hello," she said. "I'm Madhuri Singh. You must be friends of Califia's."

"Oh, sorry," Califia said. "This is Mallory MacLeod and these are Bob Andrews, Pete Crenshaw, and Jupiter Jones. I invited Mallory to see the rehearsal this afternoon. Mallory, this is our director."

Mallory shook the woman's hand. "I'm pleased to meet you," she said. "Califia told me you're great at your job."

Madhuri Singh laughed. "What a lovely accent," she said. "Scottish? It makes me feel right at home. And thank you for the kind words. Califia's been such a pleasure to work with."

"What's that dagger for?" Mallory added curiously.

Bob was glad she'd asked, since if she hadn't, Jupiter would have, and the question seemed more natural coming from Mallory. Even so, for a moment, the director didn't seem to know how to answer it. She looked startled and even confused, then dropped her voice as though she were letting the five of them in on a secret.

"It's my good luck charm," she said. "I got it in London over twenty years ago, at an antique store, when I was back in England visiting my parents. I was in the middle of my very first directing job – a student production of 'the Scottish play,' as we theater people call it. I was so nervous during rehearsals, and so superstitious – so sure that something terrible would happen. But the play went off without a hitch."

Madhuri Singh's smile grew broader. "I wasn't supposed to bring it back in my luggage, but somehow it magically made it into America. I've considered that dagger my lucky charm ever since – and I've never *ever* tried to test it by directing the Scottish play again!"

"What's the curse actually about," Califia asked, "in terms of 'the Scottish play'? I always wondered."

Pete, Jupiter, Bob, and Mallory already knew the answer, but somehow Califia didn't. Madhuri's smile faded.

"Many people think that Shakespeare stole real witches' spells for his dialogue and that, in revenge, a coven of witches put a curse on the play," she said. "Legend has it that during the very first production, a real dagger was substituted for a fake one, and the actor playing King Duncan actually died. Can you believe it?"

The surprise and shock on Califia's face were immediate.

"Oh, Califia," Madhuri Singh said, sympathetically. "Nothing bad is going to happen to you. This is *Romeo and Juliet*! Even so, I'm glad to have found my good luck charm. I must have put it down somewhere and a member of the cast or crew brought it here, thinking it was a prop."

She laughed. "As opening night approaches, I'm getting a bit more frantic, I'm afraid. We should get going," she added to Califia. "Since we're breaking this afternoon's rehearsal into four important scenes, I don't want to get behind schedule. No costumes necessary, but you and Daman should make sure you have all the props you're going to need."

"We should go," said Mallory, taking the cue. "See you after the rehearsal," she said to Califia, then led the way out of the room.

Bob followed her, and when she asked how they could get into the theater from where they were, he led the way to the door that Daman must have used that morning – a door that led to the back of the reception hall, which, in turn, led into the theater. Soon he, Pete, Jupiter, and Mallory were settling into the same row of seats the boys and Worthington had sat in earlier in the day, and soon afterwards, Daman, Califia, two other actors, and Madhuri Singh came from the wings onto the stage.

There, the only piece of stage furniture at the moment was a large low solid table, or slab, which looked like granite. A tomb, Bob knew, from having seen the movie. The actors all sat on it while Madhuri Singh made some preliminary remarks.

"Now don't forget what I told you about dramaturgy," she said kindly. "Sociologists argue that all human beings have a wide variety of *personas* they present to other people in order to persuade them to like them or trust them or help them or whatever. In sociological terms, a "dramaturgical" action is an action designed to be seen by others and – almost always – to improve a person's public image.

"The theory is that a person's identity is not stable but is constantly remade as one human being interacts with another," she went on. "That's why Romeo and Juliet find themselves acting so recklessly once they've come together. Their attraction is dangerous both to them and to the people around them, but since they've never felt like this before, they can't seem to stop themselves."

Bob found himself unexpectedly impressed with this analysis, and now he listened to Madhuri Singh tell Daman and Califia that she had cast them in the roles of Romeo and Juliet because they showed so little artifice in their daily lives, and the characters of Romeo and Juliet were almost entirely guileless. The actors were therefore an amazing match for the characters, and they should simply trust what she really had to call their *innocence* to carry them through the play.

Madhuri smiled, and concluded, "So just be yourselves."

After that, the rehearsal started, and Bob continued to be both startled and impressed by the way Madhuri Singh directed. She really trusted her young actors to understand that although there were many old-fashioned elements to the language and the action of Shakespeare's plays, the core of the stories was timeless – and in this particular story, the core of the story was that deep love led to deep grief.

Bob didn't know if Pete and Jupiter were as gripped by what they were seeing as he was, but Pete, in particular, looked riveted by Califia. In fact, after Daman had drunk the poison and died on the floor of Juliet's family tomb, and Califia had awakened to discover that her carefully-laid plans had gone terribly awry, Bob noticed that Pete was clenching his hands as Califia decided that if her husband was dead, she wanted to be dead, too. She wrenched the dagger from Romeo's belt, cried 'O happy dagger! This is thy sheath,' then arched her back and plunged the dagger into her heart.

A look of surprise and pain crossed her face. "There rust, and let me die," she said. She crumpled forward, landing half on Romeo's body.

For a moment, no one moved and nothing happened.

"Bravo, bravo!" Madhuri Singh called, applauding as she walked across the stage.

Califia sat up, smiling. "It was O.K.?" she asked.

Madhuri Singh gathered the fingers of her right hand together and kissed them. Then she hurried over and gave Califia a hug.

"And Daman!" Madhuri Singh said. "May you die like that on opening night!"

There was a great deal of congratulating all around. Everyone told Friar Lawrence how despicable he had been, to much hilarity.

"Shall we run it again?" Califia asked.

"No," Madhuri Singh said. "Why ruin perfection? Anyway, I have three other scenes to rehearse before I go home tonight. Have a good evening, everyone. See you tomorrow."

As the cast members left the stage and disappeared somewhere in the wings, Pete said, "Shouldn't we go congratulate them or something? Califia was really amazing."

"Daman was, too," Mallory said. "Even so, the whole time we were watching, I kept thinking of what had happened in the prop room, and I've finally figured out what bothered me about it. Madhuri Singh claimed she'd bought that Scottish dagger twenty years ago in London, and when I examined it, I was certain it was brand new."

Bob was struck by the truth of this observation. "That's right, you *were* certain," he said. "So what do you think that means?"

"I don't really know," Mallory said. "But I want to go online and see if I can find a similar dagger for sale. First, we should say goodbye to Daman and Califia. Then we can do some research. You have your laptop with you?"

"Yes," Bob said. "I should probably also call Worthington to tell him we're ready to be picked up." He took out his cellphone, flipped it open, and made the call; this time, he got Worthington immediately, and Worthington said he'd be at the theater in twenty minutes. Bob closed his phone and slipped it back in his pocket.

Bob frowned. "I can't imagine that Madhuri Singh was actually *lying*," he said. "She seems very professional, and I was impressed with what she said about dramaturgical theory in sociology."

"Yes," Jupiter said. "It is indisputably

true that a person's personality and even character will vary depending on who he or she is interacting with. Still, Mallory has made an excellent suggestion. I had noticed the discrepancy, too, but I hadn't come up with a plan as to how to resolve it."

Pete led the way backstage, and soon they were crowding around Daman and Califia, showering them with congratulations.

"Oh, Califia," Mallory said. "You were terrific."

"Really?" Califia said with pleasure. "Thanks so much. Some days I feel pretty confident, and other days, well – "

"You were fantastic!" Pete said. "It was hard for me to believe it was really you!"

"Well, Madhuri is a good director," Califia said, modestly.

By now, Jupiter was talking to Daman Duwalia, and from what Bob could overhear, Jupiter was saying how much he'd enjoyed the swordplay between Tybalt and Mercutio when they'd first arrived, and Daman was asking him if he'd like to come to a technical rehearsal two nights from now – there'd be lots of dueling – and Jupe was saying they'd all come, if they could.

There were goodbyes all around, and

Pete, Jupiter, Bob, and Mallory walked outside to wait for Worthington. They settled on a long wooden bench and Bob took out his laptop, booted it up, and got online; the theater's Wi-Fi extended outside. Bob was sitting between Mallory and Jupiter, and they both looked over his shoulders as he opened a browser.

"What should I try first?" he asked.

"Try Amazon," Mallory said.

Bob did, and when he got there, he typed "Scottish dirk" into the search box.

And, suddenly, there it was — the exact same dagger Bob had seen in the prop room. Bob enlarged the photo and looked at the details — the brass pommel, the damascene pattern in the steel, the leather grip on the handle.

"Although Mallory is the expert," Jupiter said, "that seems to me to be the dagger."

"Yikes!" Pete exclaimed. "And it says that it's brand new. We could get it in two days, and Madhuri Singh told us she's had it for twenty years! Maybe they've been making them that long? Or maybe it's not exactly the same?"

"But it is," Mallory said. "I'd swear on a Scottish dirk. I've already told you how I have this weird ability to remember every detail of what I see. Besides, I held that dagger in my hands. There was no wear on the grip — not a scratch or nick on the blade."

"I agree," said Jupiter. "And that means Madhuri Singh was lying."

"But why?" Bob asked.

"Why do people ever lie?" Jupiter said. "To protect themselves, cover their reputations, or fool other people into taking actions they otherwise wouldn't take. It doesn't make her a suspect, but it does mean we can't take everything she says at face value — any more than we can take everything Sir Iain says, after what we heard about him earlier."

"What did you hear?" Mallory asked.

"Please keep this in confidence," said Jupiter, "but there are rumors among the actors that Sir Iain is suffering from mental problems, and when you're investigating strange occurrences at a theater, you can't simply assume the best."

"That's true," said Bob reluctantly. "But I really, really liked him. I liked Madhuri Singh, too, and I'd bet Daman was right when he said that theaters are hotbeds of rumor and intrigue."

"The whole world is a hotbed of rumor and intrigue," said Jupiter. "And just because something is rumored to be true doesn't mean it isn't."

At that moment, the four of them caught sight of a boxy black and gray car heading up the road to the theater, and when Worthington arrived, Bob put away his laptop while Mallory retrieved her bike.

As far as Bob could remember, this would be the first time Mallory had ridden with all four of them in the Flex, and he wasn't surprised to hear Worthington invite her to sit beside him in the passenger seat after he had put her bike onto the rack. The Ford was big and roomy, but it was a tight squeeze in the back seat for three boys on the verge of turning fourteen, and it only made sense to let Mallory ride in a bit more comfort in the front.

As he settled in for the ride to the Salvage Yard, Bob thought back to the speech about dramaturgy Madhuri Singh had given. Bob had found what she'd said about a person's identity not being stable but changing in crucial ways as one human being interacted with another pretty interesting – not only because it seemed true to him, but also because *Darwin's Moral Mammals* made a similar point.

Of course, the book didn't specifically mention dramaturgical actions, but it did point out that human beings and other mammals had evolved with an instinct to deceive their fellows. In fact, it suggested that lying was an essential survival tool, and one that had led to one of the best things about human existence – the ability of people to tell and appreciate fictional tales. Without a natural instinct for lying, Shakespeare and other great writers would never have been able to hold their audiences rapt.

Up until now, Bob had been looking out the window and not paying much attention to the conversation, but as he came to the end of his train of thought, he heard Worthington say, "History is jammed with examples of people who started out well but who let their ambition run away with them."

"It's a well-trodden path, I'm afraid," Jupiter said, "and people never seem to learn. It happens over and over with tyrants and dictators. They don't start out as tyrants, but their ambition pushes them toward it."

"That's actually what *Macbeth* is all about," Mallory said.

"That's true," Worthington said. "When the play starts, Macbeth is a brave general in the army, and loyal to Duncan, the Scottish king. But when the witches prophesy that someday Macbeth will be the king himself, he believes them. Since there's only room for one king at a time, his ambition – and that of his wife – leads them to murder, then destroys them."

"Wow!" Pete said. "So what Shakespeare was really saying is that too much ambition is a curse!"

Jupiter smiled. "I guess you could say that," he said. "In any case, what we currently have are a lot of questions and very few answers. And an unusual number of suspects."

"It's Reginald Ward," Pete said darkly. "I can't wait to get him."

"We shall see," Jupiter said.

6

Jupiter Gets The Goods

The following morning, bright and early, Pete found himself at the Salvage Yard – again waiting for Worthington to pick him up, although this time with only Jupiter at his side. On the drive back from the theater the day before, Jupiter had asked Bob and Mallory to get together this morning at the library and find out everything they could about Sir Iain and Madhuri Singh, while he and Pete tried to track down the typewriter that had typed the anonymous letters.

Before they started to make the rounds of the typewriter repair shops within forty miles, Pete and Jupiter had gone to the shed in the Salvage Yard where the typewriters and similar old machines were stored. Jupe had been pretty certain that the machine they were looking for was either a manual or a portable electric, and after they brought five or six of them out to their workshop and tested them, he'd been proven right.

They'd found an old Smith Corona portable electric typewriter with what Jupiter assured Pete was a 12 point pica font and which seemed to match Daman's anonymous letters exactly. He and Jupiter had also tested an Olympia, a Royal, and a Remington; Jupiter had typed THE QUICK BROWN FOX JUMPED OVER THE LAZY DOG – the famous sentence that used every letter in the alphabet but 'S' – on all four typewriters, in both lower and upper case letters, and had compared the typed pages with the ones that Daman Duwalia had given him.

Now they were sitting in the outdoor workshop, further testing the machine – which they had set up on the table and plugged in to an outlet with an extension cord.

"If I have my dates right," Jupiter said, "this typewriter is about forty years old – give or take five years. We're lucky Uncle Titus likes typewriters. And although Aunt Mathilda tends to be somewhat intolerant about what she considers useless purchases, it seems that during the last decade, typewriters have become cool again – at least with a small subset of people."

"Why is that?" Pete asked.

"There's a backlash against digital inventions, and vinyl records, film cameras, and typewriters are all making a modest comeback," Jupiter told him.

Pete studied the typewriter with curiosity. Then, with the tip of his finger, he pressed down on the "b" key in the middle of the bottom row. He watched as the key triggered a lever that propelled a thin metal bar, arranged with others in a semicircular pattern, up and away from him. At the same time, a ribbon soaked with ink rose to meet it, and when the inverted letter on the metal bar hit the ribbon, it printed the "b" on the paper trapped between the roller Jupe had told him was called a platen and the key.

It was an ingenious invention, Pete thought, and very different from a printer. For one thing, it made a nice sociable hum as it sat there waiting for you to hit its keys; it sort of kept you company while you worked. For another, there was something reassuringly physical about typing on a typewriter. It really felt like you were *working*. You could see the result of your effort as the keys flew up and left impressions on the paper.

Pete typed some letters at random, then pulled the paper from the platen and examined it. Of course, the typewriter he and Jupiter had discovered didn't have the same signature as the one on which the anonymous letters had been written – this one had a semi-broken "o" and the "v"s and "k"s rode below the line – but Pete agreed that they were looking for a portable electric Smith-Corona.

Just then Worthington pulled up in his Mini-Cooper, and Jupiter unplugged the Smith-Corona, carried it to the Ford Flex, and set it in the back.

Worthington walked around to peer at it with interest, then the three of them got into the car. Although Pete usually rode next to him, today he didn't, since if he had, Jupiter would have had to sit in the back alone. Before Worthington arrived, Jupiter had given him the addresses of the four typewriter shops, and Worthington had programmed them into the car's GPS, so all he had to do was head for the first one, in Redwood Hills.

When the traffic noise allowed conversation, Pete – who had been thinking about Daman Duwalia – suddenly found himself saying, "Worthington, you said your mother's father was a Hindu, yes?"

"That's right," Worthington said. "A Lascar from the Indian subcontinent."

"Do you know anything about the god of death or anything like that?" Pete asked.

"I'm afraid not," Worthington replied. "My mother was raised Church of England,

and so was I. Why?”

“Daman Duwalia had some statues in his dressing room he said were representations of Hindu gods. They had four arms, and the heads of elephants and stuff,” Pete said.

“Yes,” Worthington said. “I’ve seen them. Hinduism is very theatrical. That may be why Bollywood seems so over-the-top to movie-goers from other cultures.”

“One of the anonymous letters Daman got said ‘Hollywood, Bollywood, Schmolly-wood,” Pete reported. “‘You and your lover parents are doomed to death. Remember the Thuggees?’ I thought that was pretty scary. Jupe told us about the Thuggees earlier this summer, when that crazy bear-doctor had that garrote.”

“Yes,” said Worthington. “A nasty bunch. I wonder why the letter refers to Da-man’s ‘lover’ parents? That seems a bit odd.”

“I think it’s because the parents played Romeo and Juliet in a Bollywood version of the story when they were young,” Jupiter said. “It seems that Hindu cinema has adapted *Romeo and Juliet* on any number of occasions. Unfor-tunately, I forgot to pursue the topic yesterday. I was distracted by a fire alarm going off, and by meeting Sir Iain Anthony afterwards.”

"Do you think someone could be out to get Daman because of something his parents did?" asked Pete.

"It's possible," Jupiter said. "Perhaps his father got a role someone else thought he deserved, and now he's trying to punish or frighten the son."

"Why do you say 'he'?" asked Pete curiously. "It could have been his mother who got the role."

"That's true," said Jupiter. "I should have phrased it differently."

There was silence in the car for a little while, and then Worthington looked in the rear view mirror, caught the boys' eyes, and said, "Did you like Sir Iain Anthony?"

"Very much," said Jupiter, while Pete nodded his agreement.

"I'm glad to hear that," Worthington said. "I didn't mention this when I told you I'd met him, but I have a few friends left from the days when I was acting, and two of them, independent of each other, have brought up Sir Iain in conversation recently. Each one said he'd heard Sir Iain was having difficulties."

"What kind of difficulties?" Jupiter asked.

"One of them said − and these are his words − that he'd heard that Sir Iain was 'losing his marbles,' and the other one said that he'd gotten several gossipy e-mails suggesting that the post of artistic director at the Rocky Beach Summer Theatre Festival would be vacant again soon."

"We heard something similar yesterday," Jupiter said. "From the actors who left the building during the fire alarm. I wonder where the rumors got started."

"I don't know," said Worthington. "But the friend who'd gotten the e-mails said that both his correspondents used the phrase 'that old white man' to describe Sir Iain."

When Pete thought of how nice Sir Iain had been to him and Bob and Jupiter – shaking their hands, welcoming them to the theater, saying they must be friends of Daman's, telling them something *real* about how he felt about playing villains – he felt almost literally hot under the collar.

"That's totally unfair!" he found himself blurting out. "No one decides what the color of their own skin is, and everyone eventually grows old! And, anyway, Sir Iain was such a good actor he was knighted! How many people get knighted for being really good at something? People who write stuff like 'that old white man' are as bad as whoever is writing those letters to Daman. They're trying to hurt someone who never hurt them!"

Worthington said, "Very well put, Master Crenshaw!"

Jupiter pinched his lip, looking thoughtful. "I agree with you about that phrase — which implies that being white is a bad thing, being old is a bad thing, and being both is unacceptable," he said. "But the fact remains that when a theater is rife with rumors that its artistic director is — to quote Worthington's informant — 'losing his marbles,' and you are trying to uncover the reason behind mysterious events in that very same theater, you have no choice but to consider the possibility that the two things might be connected. I, too, liked Sir Iain, but he *is* a professional actor, and if he is truly struggling with mental problems, we have to assume he'd be good at concealing them."

"Not really," Pete said. "Just because someone can act on stage doesn't mean they can act off of it."

"I agree," said Worthington. "And I've met a lot of people who can act in real life who couldn't act on a stage to save their lives."

Worthington had reached the town of Redwood Hills and was parking in front of Hutchinson's Typewriter Repair Shop. From what Pete could see, it was in a run-down neighborhood, and when the three of them went inside, they discovered that the shop was dimly lit and smelled of dust and machine oil. Jupiter was carrying the Smith-Corona when they entered.

The man behind the scratched glass counter was in his sixties, and almost bald but for a few stray hairs he combed over the top of his head. His hands were ink-stained and gnarled, but he was very friendly and ready to help if he could.

"It does me good to see a youngster with a typewriter," he said. "Let me take a look at that. Something the matter with it?"

"No," Jupiter said. "Actually, it's working fine."

"That's a good model," the man said. "Smith-Corona made a quality machine, for my money. Not many of them come my way, I can tell you."

Pete looked around the narrow store with wonder. There were typewriters every-where, and typewriter parts − belts and feet, springs and washers − in little plastic bins.

"Wow!" Pete said. "Where did you learn to work on typewriters?"

"I took one apart and put it back together when I was about your age, young man, and I was hooked. Do you have any idea how many parts there are in one typewriter?"

"A hundred?" Pete asked.

"No," the man said, smiling. "Depending on the make and model, there are between three and four thousand parts, and I have cleaned every one of them and put it back where it belongs."

"Yikes!" Pete said. "My dad's pretty handy. He's taught me how to take things apart and put them back together. But three thousand parts! That's worse than a jigsaw puzzle!"

The man laughed. "Lots of things that can go wrong," he said. "So what *can* I help you with?"

"I'm looking for another Smith Corona, like this one – with a pica font in 12 point – just in case this one goes out of commission," Jupiter said.

"You can always bring it here," the man said. "I'll be happy to fix it for you."

"Thank you," Jupiter said. "But I'd like a backup, if I can find one. So I was wondering if you might have a database of repairs you've done on a similar machine. I might be able to contact the owner and see if he or she would be willing to part with theirs."

"I'm sorry, son," the man said. "I'd help you if I could. But, as I said, it's been donkey's years since I worked on one of them. Those records are long gone."

"Well," Jupiter said. "Thank you very much anyway. Would you have a ribbon for this model?"

The man went to one of his bins and pulled out a new typewriter ribbon. "That'll be $6.99," he said. "Plus tax."

Jupiter paid the man, thanked him again, then picked up the Smith-Corona and led the way back to the car.

"Why did you buy a ribbon, Jupe?" Pete asked, perplexed.

"To cement good relations," Jupiter said. "In case I needed the man's help in future."

And then they were off to the next shop on the list – this one tucked away down an alley in Encino. The repairman there was young, in his thirties, and Pete, Jupiter, and Worthington discovered that he was a mechanical wizard of sorts – someone who instinctively understood how things were put together. He'd worked on automobile and airplane engines, refrigerators and air conditioners, copy machines and adding machines, he said. But he liked typewriters best of all.

"Nope," he said cheerfully. "Can't help you. We don't keep those kinds of records, and besides, those Smith-Coronas never break!"

Jupiter thanked him, bought a typewriter ribbon, and left.

"Jeez!" Pete said. "What are you going to do with all of those ribbons?"

"Since more and more people are going retro, they'll need ribbons for their machines. These are universal ribbons, so they'll come in handy when Aunt Mathilda starts to sell all the typewriters she wishes Uncle Titus had never bought."

The third store was in Westwood, where U.C.L.A. was, and the sidewalks around Millimeter Office Supply were filled with a young crowd. Once again, the staff was friendly but couldn't help, and it seemed to Pete that Jupiter was beginning to get both aggravated and frustrated.

Pete, too, was a little hot and tired – though he'd gotten interested enough in typewriters by that time that he didn't really mind. There was just one more shop on the list, this one in Santa Monica. Shelley's Office Emporium was, by far, the largest of the businesses they'd visited; it had the biggest selection of used typewriters and typewriter equipment, and at the back were several private offices.

Even before they were helped by a salesperson, Pete spied two Smith-Coronas very much like the one Jupiter was carrying. That would make it hard for him to say he was trying to locate another one, Pete reflected, as Jupiter set the machine he was carrying down on a glass countertop – right next to an old-fashioned ledger marked **REPAIRS** on the front.

A middle-aged man with a blue serge shirt came up behind the counter. He had a name patch with "Ernie" embroidered on it, and he looked inquiringly at Jupiter.

"If I'm not mistaken, that's a Smith-Corona Coronomatic 2500 you've got there," he said. "Looks like it's in pretty good condition. I can make it like new. Probably run you a hundred, a hundred fifty. Plus parts. I can also sell you a carrying case if you want one. At least, I think I can. The guy who owns this store has finally decided to enter the modern age, but he still hasn't got all his records on computer."

Jupiter nodded. "I know what you mean," he said. "My aunt and uncle own a salvage yard in Rocky Beach, and they've also just decided to computerize. Getting all the inventory listed is a lot of work at the beginning."

Ernie didn't seem interested in Jupiter's small talk – though Pete was. Why was Jupiter sharing this information with Ernie?

"So do you want me to recondition the thing or not?" Ernie asked.

To Pete's further surprise, Jupiter said, "Not really. I have a friend who's been receiving anonymous typed letters, and I'm trying to find the person responsible. Have you worked on any typewriters like this one?"

The man's eyes narrowed. "Maybe," he said. "I don't remember."

As he was speaking, he casually moved the ledger marked REPAIRS a little closer to him. Obviously, he *did* remember, Pete thought – and Jupiter had clearly reached the same conclusion.

"At my aunt and uncle's salvage yard, there's a section of typewriters and typewriter parts, and we'd be happy to let someone from Shelley's Office Emporium select up to $200 worth, if you help me out. If you prefer, we could pay $150 directly to the store," he said.

Wow! Pete thought. Jupiter was trying to bribe the man, straight out! He couldn't remember Jupiter ever having done this before, and he was both alarmed and impressed.

Ernie was neither. With what looked a

bit like a snarl, he said, "I don't decide about anything like that. I'd have to talk to the manager."

"Please do," said Jupiter pleasantly.

Ernie glowered at him, then turned on his heel and went to a private office at the rear of the store. The moment his back was turned, Jupiter flipped open the book that said REPAIRS and started to examine its entries. While Pete watched the door of the office into which Ernie had vanished, Jupiter ran his finger down column after column of handwritten entries until he stabbed his finger on one particular one and stopped.

Pete was so intent on watching for Ernie's return that he didn't want to look over to see exactly what Jupiter was doing, but he heard him close the REPAIRS book and slide it back to where it had been on the counter. "It's O.K., Pete," he said. "You can relax. I got it."

Pete was very glad to hear that, because Ernie had now emerged from the office at the back, and was heading toward them, accompanied by a man who looked even angrier than Ernie did.

"Let's go before they get here!" Pete hissed, but Jupiter said in a low voice, "There's something else I need to say."

When the men arrived, Jupiter smiled at them pleasantly but a little stupidly. "Just who do you think you are, kid?" the manager said.

Jupiter was good at looking stupid when he wanted to, Pete thought. It was the last remaining evidence of his early career as a child actor, and it came in very handy in situations like this one.

At last the manager stopped talking about customer confidentiality and the reputation of the store and the fact that he was thinking of calling the police and reporting Jupiter for attempted bribery long enough for Jupiter to get a word in edgewise. Well, really a whole lot of words, Pete reflected.

"I don't know what you're talking about, sir," Jupiter said, looking a bit offended. "I told Ernie that my aunt and uncle own a salvage yard in Rocky Beach, and that Shelley's Office Emporium might want to take a look at its old typewriters sometime. I said it was amazing what you could get there for $200. I also told him that $150 was a good price for a total typewriter recondition."

Ernie looked as if he were going to explode, but the manager started to look doubtful.

"Well, Jupe," Pete said decisively, "It's

time for us to go now."

Without waiting for Jupiter to answer, he grabbed the Smith- Corona off the counter and headed for the exit. Jupiter followed, and soon Pete was putting the typewriter into the Ford Flex, and he and Jupiter were climbing into the back seat. Worthington turned the engine on and pulled back onto the street while Pete turned to Jupiter. "All right! Tell us! You said you got it! What did you get?" he said.

Jupiter looked at him almost as if he were unhappy. "A Smith-Corona Coronomatic 2500 was brought in for repair a month ago. The cost of the repair was $100. The name of the person who brought the machine into the shop was Reginald Ward. An uncommon name, in my experience."

"Reginald Ward?" Pete exclaimed in astonishment. "You mean the guy who's playing Tybalt? The guy who came storming into the prop room, insulted Daman Duwalia, then called us rug-rats? Rug-rats! I'd like to rug-rat *him!* Of *course* it would be him writing all those nasty letters! You *said* he was jealous of Daman's fame! Well, this explains everything! Good work, Jupe! You really got the goods!"

To Pete's surprise, as they turned back onto the highway heading for Rocky Beach,

Jupiter continued to look unhappy. "Daman told us that Reginald Ward is somehow related to Sir Iain," Jupiter said. "Presuming this *is* the Reginald Ward playing Tybalt, he could have simply been bringing a typewriter owned by Sir Iain in for repair. Sir Iain is much more likely to own such a thing, and although I like Sir Iain as much as you do, I'm afraid that he and his distant relative have just *both* become suspects in this case."

"Gosh," said Pete. "I guess that's true."

"Also, I wish you hadn't called me Jupe in front of Ernie and the manager," Jupiter said. "I was thinking on my feet, but even so, I was an idiot to tell Ernie that my aunt and uncle owned a salvage yard in Rocky Beach. That alone would have been enough to lead him to my identity, but if you add 'Jupe' into the mix, we might as well have handed them a Three Investigators card."

"Jeez," Pete said. "I'm sorry, Jupe." He was silent for a moment, then added, "But the main thing is that now we know who's been writing the letters! I'm *sure* it wasn't Sir Iain; it *must* have been Reginald Ward. Don't you think so, Worthington?"

"I don't have enough information to make a judgment yet," Worthington said. "And you and Jupiter still need to find the typewriter."

"That's true," Jupiter agreed. "But first I want to find out more about Sir Iain, and I've been thinking that maybe Charlotte Mitchell can help us. When we met her at the theater, she said she works for Sir Iain just the way she works for Isabella Chang. Although we couldn't ask her to reveal any confidences, she might be willing to shed some light on Sir Iain's relationship with Reginald Ward."

"That's true!" said Pete. "And I like her!"

"You like almost everyone," said Jupiter, grinning. "You probably even liked André Laurent when he was holding a knife to your throat."

"Oh, no, I didn't," Pete said. "Though I felt sorry for him when the police hauled him off in their cruiser. Anyway, maybe we could call Charlotte and ask her if we could talk to her right away."

"Great idea, Second," Jupiter said.

"Bob has her number programmed into his phone, but he's not here," Pete added.

"I have a good memory for numbers, and Charlotte's is especially easy," Jupiter said. "I don't have it programmed into my phone, but when I knew we would be coming out without Bob today, I brought my phone with me."

"Good thinking, Jupe!" said Pete. He almost never thought of bringing his own phone – although he had one. He just didn't like them, somehow – and he didn't much like computers, either. Maybe that was why he'd been so fascinated by his introduction to typewriters; in fact, if he was a little older, maybe he'd be one of those people who went retro.

Pete watched as Jupiter pulled his phone out of his pocket and flipped it open. He dialed Charlotte Mitchell's number and she picked up after two rings. Pete couldn't hear Charlotte's half of the conversation but from Jupiter's half, he gathered she was at Isabella Chang's house, and that if he and Pete wanted to come by, both she and Isabella would be happy to see them.

7

A Visit To Isabella Chang's

Isabella Chang lived on a cul-de-sac in the southern part of Rocky Beach, and about ten minutes later, Jupiter stood next to Pete as his friend pushed her doorbell enthusiastically. Pete was obviously still excited about the discovery of Reginald Ward's name in the repairs book at Shelley's Office Emporium, but although Jupiter was glad to have gotten such a solid lead in just three or four hours of legwork, Pete's excitement was almost certainly premature.

As Worthington had pointed out, until The Three Investigators were able to locate the actual typewriter on which the anonymous letters had been typed, they really had nothing. All they knew was that someone named Reginald Ward had dropped off and picked up a typewriter from Shelley's Office Emporium – a typewriter on which the threatening letter might have been written.

But the same could be said for every other Smith-Corona in southern California; at the moment, they didn't even have proof that the Reginald Ward who was playing Tybalt and the Reginald Ward who had brought in a Smith-Corona Coronomatic 2500 were one and the same person.

Of course, there *had* been an address and a phone number next to his name, but all Jupiter had had time to see was that the address had been in Los Angeles.

In fact, the only thing that had *really* changed as a result of the long, hot morning was that there now seemed a very real possibility that Reginald Ward had brought a typewriter owned by Sir Iain in for repair – and that Sir Iain himself was the author of the anonymous letters.

After all, the notes had mentioned Bollywood, the Thugees, and the Hindu god of death, and somehow Jupiter didn't see references like these stocking the mind of Reginald Ward. Even the combining of a famous line from *Macbeth* with a famous line from *Romeo and Juliet* seemed a bit challenging for what was, on the evidence so far, a fairly basic brain.

As Jupiter stood, shifting his weight from foot to foot, he was also feeling worried that he might have reacted too quickly to Pete's suggestion that they contact Charlotte Mitchell – or at least that he hadn't thought quickly enough when she'd told him she was at Isabella Chang's.

He, Pete, and Bob had met Isabella when she'd hired The Three Investigators to research an ancestor of hers, and since she'd assume that the reason he and Pete were coming to her house was to talk with *her*, it would be rude, Jupiter thought, to let her see that he and Pete had really come to ask Charlotte about Sir Iain.

At last he heard the sound of hurrying footsteps, and the door flew open. The first time The Three Investigators had met Charlotte – on this very same doorstep – she had worn such eccentric and colorful clothing that Pete had wondered aloud if she had a sideline as a fortuneteller. Today she wore a gauzy white shirt with puffy sleeves, a skirt that looked as if it had started off as a quilt, and a clamor of gold and silver bangles around her wrists.

"What a nice surprise that you called," she said. "Come in! Isabella is waiting by the koi pond with some iced tea and lemonade."

Jupiter was hot and tired enough after the morning's endeavors that he was glad to follow Charlotte through the house and into the back yard. There Isabella sat waiting. Although at least one of her ancestors had been from

Ireland, she looked entirely Chinese, and although she was in her mid-80s, she had the energy and stamina of a much younger woman. She had great physical presence and real vitality.

"Hello, my friends," she said. "Lovely to see you. But where is Bob? I thought it was a law that the three of you were always together."

"Bob is doing research today," Jupiter said. "He'll be sorry to miss seeing you. Thank you for letting us stop by on such short notice."

In the midst of his other worries, it hadn't occurred to Jupiter that Isabella and Charlotte didn't yet know he'd discovered a number of long-lost relatives of his mother on the last Three Investigators case. So he was surprised when Pete said, "I know Bob wanted to tell you himself, but he helped Jupiter find a bunch of relations on our last case, up in Jackson. A great aunt, a first cousin once removed, and some second cousins. He used the same genealogical website he used to research Li Chang."

"Really?" Isabella Chang said with great interest. "Knowing the pleasure your discoveries about my long-dead relative have brought to me, I can hardly imagine your feelings at finding actual, living family!"

"It was fantastic," Pete agreed. "The second cousins are twins named Luke and Harper, and they have goats named Penny and Zoe."

By this time, Pete had helped himself to a drink, grabbed a few cookies, and settled himself in a chair, and now Jupiter did the same. Although meeting his maternal relations had been an extraordinary experience, at the moment all Jupiter's thoughts were on the current case.

So he simply said, "Your generous reward let us buy a car to get around California. Without it, I would never have met the twins. So I'm grateful to you on *two* counts. Right now, we're involved in a case that involves the Rocky Beach Summer Theatre Festival. I'm sorry we can't give you the details, but at the moment it's confidential."

"I understand," Isabella said. "But I should tell you that even before you boys made me a very rich woman, I'd been a longtime patron of the Festival. In fact, when you were up in Auburn, I went to the Gala to celebrate the theater's reopening. Charlotte went with me. It was mostly a thank-you to everyone who had contributed to the renovation, but it was also a chance for me to meet Sir Iain Anthony. It was an odd evening, I have to say."

"Odd?" Jupiter asked. "In what way?"

"Well, during the second half of the evening we toured the newly renovated theater buildings, then enjoyed a rather lavish reception – champagne and canapés and lots of desserts. But before that, everyone sat in the theater, and the directors of three of this summer's plays gave very brief speeches. The third one was by the Indian woman who's directing *Romeo and Juliet*."

"Madhuri Singh," Charlotte interjected.

"Yes, Madhuri Singh," said Isabella, nodding. "All three directors were impressive, but she was particularly charming. She said she'd been born in London but had grown up in Stratford-on-Avon and had gone to the Stratford theater to see Shakespeare performed when she was a girl of ten and eleven and twelve. She said that no one should underestimate the formative impact of live theater on young people, and that her life had been changed forever by her experiences in Stratford.

"Then she said that she'd never had the chance to meet Sir Iain Anthony when he was playing Macbeth or Hamlet in Stratford-on-

Avon but had had to wait until he was appointed the artistic director of a theater festival in faraway California. She said some very nice things about him, then introduced him as the final speaker of the evening."

Although Jupiter was interested to learn that Madhuri Singh had lived in Stratford-on-Avon as a girl, nothing Isabella had reported seemed strange in any way.

"So far, there's nothing odd about what you're reporting," Jupiter said. "What happened that you found odd?"

"I don't know if Charlotte would agree with me," said Isabella, "but it seemed to me that the moment Sir Iain took the podium, the atmosphere in the theater changed. I once took my tenth-grade history class on a field trip to Los Angeles to see Iain Anthony perform in *Henry V*, so I know from personal experience how great he was as an actor.

"But when he started talking on the night of the Gala, I began to feel uneasy. His voice sounded thin and reedy and annoying − like screeches on a blackboard, really. It was almost as if the microphone had been badly adjusted − though it had worked fine with the directors. I started feeling apprehensive. I think I even took Charlotte's hand."

"You did," said Charlotte, nodding. "And you know, now that you mention it, I'd have to agree with you. There was something strange about the microphone – and also about the lighting. Because of Isabella's eyesight, we were seated in the front, so I could see Sir Iain clearly, and although he is still amazingly handsome, the lighting seemed to emphasize the stiffness of his facial muscles."

"It wasn't just the lighting or the sound," said Isabella. "They say that when you start losing the use of one of your senses, your other senses can become more acute, and if there's a sense that tells you about danger, then *that's* the sense that was heightened for me while Sir Iain was on the stage. I didn't feel that *he* was in danger, I felt that *I* was. The whole time he was speaking I got more and more anxious, and although he didn't talk long, by the time he was finished, I felt like I wanted to get up and run out of the theater. It was totally irrational. A sort of irrational panic."

Jupiter looked at Isabella gravely. By now, he knew her well enough to know she would never be saying what she was saying if things hadn't happened just as she described. A lifetime of teaching history to high school stu-dents had taught her to be very precise – almost scientific – in both her observations and her remarks.

"I don't think I was the only one who felt that way, either," she added. "Since Charlotte works for Sir Iain, she probably wasn't quite as susceptible as the rest of us, but I thought the relief was almost palpable when Sir Iain was done. After we'd all seen the renovations and gathered for refreshments, I heard people around me saying that maybe Sir Iain should have stayed retired."

"No!" said Charlotte. "I didn't hear that! Sir Iain is wonderful, just wonderful. So warm, and so generous. You couldn't meet a nicer man."

"I agree with you," Isabella said. "When you introduced us at the reception, he seemed like a totally different person from the one who'd been speaking on the stage. His voice was rich and vibrant – a pleasure to listen to – and he had a warmth about him that was reassuring and even inviting, not frightening. Even so, when he was on the stage, I wanted to run away, and from the conversations around me at the reception, I could tell that other people had wanted to do the same."

"I see why you called it an odd experience," Jupiter said. "It's very odd."

It also reminded him of something —
though at the moment he couldn't remember
what.

He sat and thought for a minute, then
asked Isabella, "Did you meet a young man
named Reginald Ward that evening? He's
playing Tybalt in *Romeo and Juliet*, and I understand that he's somehow related to Sir Iain. A
surly sort."

"I didn't meet him, no," said Isabella.

"He's Sir Iain's daughter-in-law's
nephew," Charlotte said, unexpectedly. "And
he really isn't as bad as he seems. He has a
chip on his shoulder because he knows he's not
a very good actor, and his aunt married Sir
Iain's son when Reg was still young enough to
hope he could be. Even so, he's kind to Sir
Iain. He seems truly grateful for the opportuni-
ties he's given him, and runs errands for him
from time to time. Being directed by Madhuri
Singh seems to bring out the worst in him."

"That can happen," Isabella said, nodding. "Certain people can have a very unfortunate effect on others."

"I was recently thinking something like
that myself," Jupiter said. He turned to Charlotte. "How long have you known Madhuri
Singh? And what do you know about her?"

"I've known her for seven or eight years," Charlotte said. "As I told you, I've been working at the theater in the summers for a long time now, and she's been directing the yearly summer Shakespeare production maybe half that time. As Isabella said, she was born in London but grew up in Stratford-on-Avon, and then went to college in California. I don't know how she got into television, but except when she's directing Shakespeare, she's a television producer. A quite successful one, I think."

"Really?" Pete said curiously. "She doesn't seem hard-nosed enough for that. My dad told me that producers have to be really ruthless if they want to succeed in the film industry."

"I don't know much about it," Charlotte said. "But I agree that she doesn't seem very ruthless. "

"What other plays has she directed?" asked Jupiter.

Since Madhuri Singh had also become a suspect when Bob confirmed that she'd lied about the age of her dagger, he wanted to take this opportunity to learn as much as possible about her. Luckily, asking Charlotte about Madhuri had flowed naturally out of the conversation.

"Well, last year the theater was closed, of course, for renovations," Charlotte said, "but the year before that, she directed *Midsummer Night's Dream*, and she's also done *As You Like It*, *The Tempest*, and *Twelfth Night*. *Romeo and Juliet* is the first tragedy she's directed."

"Tragedies aren't generally considered a wise choice for summer theater," Isabella said. "But I suppose that Madhuri Singh may be running out of other choices, and *Romeo and Juliet* can be considered a love story, in a certain light."

Jupiter was about to ask if Madhuri Singh was married when Charlotte said, "Actually, Madhuri wanted to do *Macbeth* this season. She pushed quite hard for it."

Jupiter sat up straight.

"Of course, it was totally the wrong sort of play for summer in Rocky Beach, but she seemed so eager to do a tragedy that Sir Iain finally agreed to let her do *Romeo and Juliet*, instead."

"Is that so?" Jupiter said thoughtfully. When Mallory had asked Madhuri Singh about the Scottish dirk, she'd said she'd gotten it in London as a good luck charm when she was directing *Macbeth*, and that she'd never tried to test it by directing the play again.

While Jupiter supposed that, technically, a failed attempt to get permission to direct the play wouldn't contradict what she had said, it did seem that there were now *two* lies which might be laid at her feet – and both of them had been uttered during the same conversation.

"Is there anything else you can tell us about her?" he said to Charlotte.

"Not really," she said. "Except that I thought she acted very decently when Sir Iain got the job of artistic director."

"Why shouldn't she?" asked Pete. "I'd think any director would be happy to have him as a boss."

"I agree," Charlotte said. "All I meant was that since she applied for the position, too, she must have felt a little disappointed when Sir Iain got it, instead."

"Madhuri Singh applied to be the artistic director of the Rocky Beach Summer Theatre Festival?" Jupiter said.

"Three years ago, the Festival's director – a local woman who'd held the post for nine years – decided to retire. The search for her replacement came down to three finalists, and although Madhuri Singh had an established history with the theater, the board decided that Sir Iain should be the artistic director – citing his long and distinguished career."

And, Jupiter thought, his connections with many people with very deep pockets. It had been a prudent decision – one you couldn't argue with – and it had worked out well for all concerned. Unless, of course, the rumors about Sir Iain were actually true, he thought.

Jupiter glanced at his watch and decided it was time to wrap this visit up. For one thing, Worthington was waiting to take them back to the Salvage Yard, and for another, Jupiter had never quite relaxed about the possibility that Isabella Chang might figure out that he and Pete hadn't really stopped by to visit *her*.

"Well," he said. "I suppose we should go. Thank you for the refreshments, and the interesting information."

"Do you want to see our new car before we leave?" Pete said to Isabella suddenly. "After all, we said we'd take you for a ride in it sometime."

"I'd love to see it," Isabella said, getting to her feet. "Why don't we both go, Charlotte?"

Together, they started walking toward the front door. Pete and Jupiter followed as Isabella and Charlotte led the way through the house. At the closed door to the wing, Isabella paused and smiled slyly.

"I hope you haven't forgotten your search for my new housemate," she said.

"No," Jupiter said. "We're keeping our eyes open."

In the front yard, Worthington was leaning against the Flex reading a newspaper, but when the four of them came out of the house, he straightened, and Jupiter introduced him to Isabella Chang.

"How do you do, Ms. Chang," said Worthington. "I've heard a lot about you – all of it good! It seems we have in common an admiration for the youngest investigators in the Los Angeles area."

"Yes, indeed," Isabella said. "I've taught a lot of young people in my time, and Pete and Bob and Jupiter would stand out in any class."

She looked beyond Worthington to the gray Ford Flex with the black top. "And that looks like the perfect car for them," she added.

"Come on!" said Pete. "You've got to see the chimera decal on the back. It's a single animal with three heads!"

"Just like The Three Investigators," said Isabella sagely.

"That's exactly what *I* thought!" Pete exclaimed. "And now an artist friend called

Connor O'Malley has designed a chimera especially for us. We met him up in Auburn."

He stopped and looked at Charlotte. "You know," he said, "I think you'd really like him, and he'd like you. Don't you think so, Jupe?"

Though Jupiter had no opinion on the subject, he nodded. "Very possibly," he said.

Then, while Charlotte talked to Worthington, Isabella examined the chimera decal – after which Charlotte joined her to peer at it, too. She admired it, then looked past it into the back of the car, and when she saw the Smith Corona Coronomatic 2500 sitting on the black carpeting, she said in a tone of great surprise, "Why, that's Sir Iain's typewriter! What's it doing in your car? Is it broken again? He loves that machine! And he can still type on it, too."

"Really?" Jupiter asked.

"He likes to send hand-typed notes to old friends. He can't write by hand any more, but he's had that machine so long it's like an old friend itself. Why do you have it in your car?" Charlotte asked again.

"We don't," Jupiter said. "This machine belongs to my Aunt Mathilda and my Uncle Titus, and I'm afraid I can't tell you why it's here without breaching the confidentiality of a client."

Jupiter could see that Pete was almost bursting with the desire to do just that, but he reined himself in.

After saying their goodbyes, Worthington, Pete, and Jupiter climbed into the car and started for the Salvage Yard. The minute they were safely out of the driveway, Pete started saying that, in spite of what Charlotte had said, he still thought Reginald Ward had taken the opportunity, when Sir Iain had asked him to have his typewriter repaired, to type up a bunch of threatening, nasty notes to a director he disliked and a fellow actor he was jealous of.

But while Jupiter had to admit that this was possible, he was more focused on how many different factors in the current investigation seemed to point to Sir Iain Anthony. Of course, there were also reasons to distrust Madhuri Singh and to wonder about Reginald Ward, but even so, Jupiter had to acknowledge glumly that Sir Iain might well be suffering from dementia, and if he was, might be capable of doing things he would never have done before he got ill.

Still, what bothered Jupiter most at the moment was that part of him was certain Isabella Chang had told him and Pete something important – something *really* important – but as he sat in the car being driven back to the Salvage Yard, he had absolutely no idea what it was.

8

Mallory Makes Some Inroads

Bob had agreed to meet Mallory at the Rocky Beach Public Library at 10:00 that morning and had just secured his bike and taken off his helmet when she pedaled up. Ever since he'd met her, Mallory had been scornful of California's law that bicyclists under the age of 18 were supposed to wear a helmet. But today she was wearing one – one that looked a lot like the climbing helmet Bob had checked out from the Rocky Beach High School sports program.

This didn't really surprise him, since the first time he and she had ever talked – on the steps of the Rocky Beach Library, coincidentally enough – Mallory had told him that the only time she'd ever worn a helmet had been when she'd gone climbing in Scotland with her father. That was what had given him the idea to ask if she'd like to go climbing in Palisade Point sometime – and now might be a good time to do that.

"You've got your climbing helmet on!" he said.

"Just until I can get a bike one," Mallory said, locking her bike next to Bob's. "In Scotland, I always felt safe riding on country roads, but California is full of lunatics. I just ran into a few of them. Well not ran *into*, thankfully. But they seemed to want to run into *me*," she said. She took the helmet off, and shook her hair out.

"I've got a climbing helmet, too," Bob said. "I've chosen climbing as my sport for our freshman year, and I checked out some gear. I was thinking of trying the cliffs outside of Palisade Point."

"Where's Palisade Point?" asked Mallory, as she led the way toward the steps of the library.

"On the coast about forty-five minutes from here," Bob said. "Maybe we could go climbing there together before school starts."

"I've never climbed with anyone but my father," said Mallory. "I don't know. I'll have to think about it. Maybe."

For a moment, Bob felt disappointed, but when Mallory swung open the heavy library door, she smiled at him in such an openhearted way that he felt hopeful that 'maybe' might turn into 'yes.' In the meantime, he had nothing to complain about; he was glad that Jupiter had suggested that he and Mallory come to the library this morning and find out everything they could about Sir Iain and Madhuri Singh.

Since they both had laptops, they could have gone somewhere else, but as they made their way to a table where they could talk quietly without disturbing anyone, Bob was pleased they'd come here.

He pulled a chair out and sat down. "Maybe I can start with Sir Iain and you can start with Madhuri Singh?"

"Great," Mallory said. "And then we can compare notes." She took her laptop out of her backpack and set it on the table. She also unpacked a pen and a pad of lined paper.

Bob got out his own laptop and flipped it open. "At this point, I'm more suspicious of Madhuri Singh than of Sir Iain," he said.

"Me, too," Mallory said. "When someone lies to your face the way Madhuri Singh did, you've got good reason to suspect her of being up to something."

Miss Bennett, the head librarian at the library and also Bob's boss, wiggled her fingers at him as she walked by, and he waved back.

"Jupiter said people lie to protect themselves, cover their reputations, or fool other people into doing something they wouldn't do otherwise," he said. "I wonder what Madhuri Singh's reason was."

"Well, it wasn't to protect herself," Mallory said. "I guess it could have been to cover her reputation, but I can't imagine why she would have been embarrassed to own a dagger that *wasn't* a so-called 'lucky dagger.'"

Bob nodded and got onto the library's Wi-Fi.

"That leaves the last one," he said. "In this case, paying no attention to the dagger."

"Of course, if Madhuri Singh had known we knew it was magnetized, she might not have thought she could make us forget it by coming up with a plausible story about directing *Macbeth*," Mallory said.

"Gosh, that's right, isn't it?" Bob said. "I wonder if *she* knew it was magnetized. If she did, it could be the clue to the entire case. That she was lying *because* it was magnetized – and she knew it."

"Yes," Mallory said. "Though I really can't see how it connects to the anonymous letters Daman's been getting, or the story he told you about those Hindu statues."

Bob, Pete, and Jupiter had related this story in the car the day before.

"Well, shall we get started?" Bob said.

"Absolutely," Mallory said, and they turned to their computers. When Bob typed "Sir Iain Anthony" into the search box on his browser, there were close to a million results. That made him smile. He thought he probably wouldn't check all of them out, but he quickly discovered that Sir Iain had his own website, and, of course, there were articles about him on Wikipedia and the Internet Movie Database. There were also hundreds of interviews with him, both in English and American papers.

Bob decided to limit his search to the last ten years, and after spending about half an hour reading interview after interview – a lot of them touching on his Parkinson's disease and his disappointment about having to retire from acting – he stumbled upon an article written about ten years before.

Across the table he saw Mallory scribbling notes to herself on her lined paper pad, but he had just been bookmarking articles he thought he might go back to. This one was in a London paper, about Iain Anthony being knighted. Since he'd begun his career at the theater in Stratford-on-Avon where he'd played many of Shakespeare's tragic heroes, the paper had interviewed people connected to the theater who had known him in his early days.

It was a long article and there were lots of people quoted, but Bob was most interested in the remarks of a man named Arjun Singh. He was an accountant for the theater who, along with his wife, had emigrated to England from India and who'd been amazed to be offered a job in Stratford-on-Avon. He said that even though he worked with numbers for a living, and planned to return to India when he retired, he'd always loved both Great Britain and Shakespeare.

In the article, Arjun Singh proudly told a story about introducing his eleven-year-old daughter to Iain Anthony after he'd taken her to see a production of *Macbeth*. According to Mr. Singh, his daughter had been electrified and had wanted to meet the actor who had played the title role. He'd been very kind to her, and when it turned out she'd forgotten her autograph book, had told her to come back another night so that he could sign it. He called his daughter "Dhuri" and Bob found himself wondering whether the girl could have been Madhuri Singh.

He looked up both "Madhuri" and "Singh" and when he discovered they were common Indian names, he supposed that Arjun Singh's daughter might have been a different person than the one Mallory was currently researching just across the table. He made a mental note to look into the issue further, then found a series of articles about Sir Iain Anthony much closer to home – in the Rocky Beach *Herald*.

Like too many articles in his hometown paper, they were poorly written and a bit confusing. Nevertheless, when Bob read them in order, a story emerged. Three years before, the Rocky Beach Summer Theatre Festival's artistic director had decided to step down. As it turned out, the search for her replacement had gone on for much of a year and had come down to three finalists for the position. Bob was surprised to see that one of the three had been Madhuri Singh.

In fact, he was so surprised that he couldn't help himself. He pushed his laptop aside and whispered, "Mallory!"

She looked up at him. "What?" she said.

"I just found out that when Sir Iain was chosen as the artistic director of the theater there were two other finalists. And Madhuri Singh was one of them."

"I know!" Mallory said, a bit more loudly than she'd meant to, Bob saw. She quieted down. "I found that out, too. And then I found out something even more interesting. Madhuri Singh might have met Sir Iain when she was a girl in England. I had to look hard to find out where she grew up, and when she came to America and so on, but she was born in London and moved to Stratford-on-Avon with her parents when she was still quite young."

Bob was oddly excited. "Her father was an accountant for the theater," he said. "I found an article that had an interview with him. I didn't know for sure he *was* her father, but now I do! Do you want me to send you a link to the article?"

"Yes," Mallory said. It was shortly loading on her computer. She read it quickly, but in silence. When she was done, she sat back and crossed her arms.

"According to her father, Madhuri Singh was just a star-struck eleven-year-old girl who wanted to meet her idol," she said. "But in light of our current investigation, that meeting raises an interesting question. Could either Madhuri Singh or Sir Iain have a grudge of some sort that goes back all those years?"

"What kind of grudge could an eleven-year-old girl have against an actor playing

Macbeth?" Bob asked. "Or vice versa, for that matter? Over the years, Sir Iain must have met so many fans and signed so many autographs, it's hard to imagine him even remembering the meeting."

"Because Sir Iain loomed so large in her imagination, Madhuri Singh couldn't have forgotten meeting *him*," Mallory said. "Maybe I shouldn't have said a grudge. Maybe Arjun Singh got the story wrong. Maybe Madhuri was actually *frightened* by *Macbeth* – traumatized at the murderous nature of the character. Maybe she mixed up the actor with the character – or maybe he did something frightening when she met him. Could she be trying to get back at Sir Iain by making bad things happen in his theater?"

"But it's not Sir Iain the bad things are happening to," Bob said. "It's Madhuri Singh and Daman Duwalia."

"I know," said Mallory, suddenly looking frustrated. "But we both think that Madhuri Singh's lie about the dagger trumps the rumors about Sir Iain. The thing is, I'm a pretty good liar myself. I don't like people telling me what to do, and being told never to lie just makes me want to do it. Luckily, I've always been smart enough to keep myself out of serious trouble."

Bob wasn't sure what she was leading up to, but he felt flattered by her frankness. After all, all human beings lied. The motive behind the lie – and whether it did any real damage – were the things that really mattered.

"And, of course," Mallory added, "my ability came in handy when I told Daniel Hernández I was hoping to become his student the day I went to his office to try to get a copy of the Kit Carson letter. If I hadn't pretended I was someone I wasn't, I could never have fooled him into giving me important information."

"Vital information," Bob said. He suddenly remembered what Madhuri Singh had said about the wide variety of *personas* everyone had inside and how a dramaturgical action was an action designed to be seen by others.

"It wasn't really vital," Mallory said modestly. "But the point I was making is that since I'm good at deceiving people when I want to, I'm also good at figuring out when people are deceiving me. And there's more to Madhuri Singh's dagger than meets the eye."

"Pete and Jupe ought to be back by now," Bob said. "Maybe we should bike over to the Salvage Yard and trade information."

"Yes, let's go," Mallory said.

They closed their laptops, stuffed them in their backpacks, and waved goodbye to Miss Bennett. When they got to the Salvage Yard, they found that Pete and Jupiter were, indeed, back, and as Mallory and Bob pulled up on their bikes, Pete – who was bursting with excitement – started to talk at once.

"Wait 'til you hear what we found out!" he said. "I told you it was Reginald Ward! He brought a typewriter exactly like the one we're looking for into a repair shop in Santa Monica! And on the way back we stopped off to talk to Charlotte Mitchell. She was at Isabella Chang's and she told us that there's a typewriter just like the one that was used to type the anonymous letters in Sir Iain's office, and that he still uses it!"

"Why don't we continue this conversation in the outdoor workshop?" Jupiter suggested. He led the way there, and when they'd all settled down, Pete continued his explanation.

"Jupiter thinks it could be Sir Iain – because it's his typewriter and because he may be suffering from something mental – but I think it has to be Reginald Ward. Charlotte told us he has a chip on his shoulder because he's a terrible actor."

"Actually, Charlotte tried to steer us away from Reginald," Jupiter said. "She also told us quite a bit about Madhuri Singh."

"Did she tell you that Madhuri Singh grew up in Stratford-on-Avon?" Bob asked. He was eager to fill Jupiter and Pete in on what he and Mallory had discovered, but just as he was about to go on, he heard a car turn into the Salvage Yard.

He looked up to see a low-slung cherry-red convertible with protruding headlights and creamy ivory upholstery screech to a halt, skidding on the gravel, coming uncomfortably close to The Three Investigators' Ford Flex. Although the workshop was partly screened off, they could all see clearly enough who had just arrived.

"Oh, no," Mallory groaned. "What on earth can *he* want?"

"Nothing good," said Pete, as he and Jupiter jumped to their feet. Bob and Mallory followed as E. Skinner Norris slowly extricated himself from the driver's seat.

"Hello, Mally-Wally," he said. "And The Three Little Investigators! Long time, no see."

"Not long enough," Pete said.

Skinny tilted back his head so that his chin was pointing at the four of them, and from that angle he looked down his nose. His hair, which had recently been cut to less than a half inch, bristled all over the crown of his egg-shaped head, and Bob could see his white scalp through it. His Adam's apple bobbed up and down as he swallowed. Bob had always disliked him, but right now he found Skinny's condescending self-righteousness really unbearable.

"McSherlock," Skinny said to Jupiter. "I just received the most alarming information."

Jupiter remained silent, though he raised his eyebrows.

"I was with my bro Reginald Ward – "

"That guy is friends with you?" Pete exploded. "I should have known! You're two of a kind!"

Skinny swatted the air in front of him as though Pete were a bothersome gnat.

" – and Reg got a call from a man named Ernie. Is the name familiar? Some drone at an office supply store in Santa Monica?"

"Oh, no," Pete groaned. Jupiter's face remained impassive. He was giving nothing away. He shook his head at Pete to let him know he shouldn't say anything else. Bob wondered what could be going on.

"Anyway," Skinny continued, "Ernie has some loser brother who thinks he's ready to be a stunt man." He snorted. "Ha ha ha! Ernie thought in return for some information Reg could give his loser brother a hand breaking into films." Skinny was clearly enjoying himself.

"This is all very interesting," Jupiter said. "But what does it have to do with us?"

"According to Ernie, a certain 'Jupe'" – Skinny said the name with a sneer – "from a certain 'Salvage Yard' in Rocky Beach was in earlier today, and wanted information about Reg. When Ernie balked, this 'Jupe' tried to bribe him – "

"He did not!" Pete yelled. "It was all a trick. Jupiter wanted to find out – "

"Thank you, Pete," Jupiter said. "I'll take it from here."

"As you might expect, McSherlock, it doesn't take even a kiddie detective to figure out that the only 'Jupe' who lives in a Rocky Beach junkyard is you."

"That is undoubtedly true," said Jupiter mildly.

"It isn't a junkyard, it's a salvage yard!" Pete said.

"Well, whatever it's called, according to

my dictionary, what you offered to loser Ernie was a bribe," Skinny said.

"When was the last time you were within a hundred miles of a dictionary?" Bob asked.

"So?" Skinny said to Jupiter. "Always so high-and-mighty. Always so earnest and logical and honest. Now you've shown your true colors, McSherlock."

"Ernie misheard me," Jupiter said, "and jumped to the wrong conclusion. I was merely telling him how much value he could get at the Salvage Yard, on the one hand, and complimenting him on his reasonable charge for a typewriter overhaul, on the other. Rather than ask for clarification, he dragged his manager into the fracas, but the manager quickly saw who was in the wrong."

"Oh yeah?" Skinny said, taken aback. The freight train of his condescension was momentarily shunted off onto a side track and lost steam.

"You're just jealous!" Pete said. "You've always been jealous of Jupiter."

"Jealous?" Skinny said haughtily. "Why should I be jealous of someone who lives behind a junkyard?" he said.

"Well," Bob said. "Let me count the ways. Because he's way smarter than you? And better looking? And because he has friends? And he gets things done?"

"And because he has a purpose in life," Mallory said, "instead of tooling around in a ridiculous car and making trouble for people?"

Skinny pulled himself together and made one final assault.

"You can take all that and stuff it," he snapped. "Reggie isn't happy. He's thinking of reporting you to the authorities."

"I've always wondered," Jupiter said, "what your first initial stands for, Skinny. Now that you've decided to be the watchdog of propriety, perhaps you've earned the right to be called something more elevated than 'Skinny'. So what's your first name? Ezekiel?"

"No," Skinny sputtered. "Not even close."

"Maybe you're an Ernie, too," Bob said. "Fellow travelers."

"Elijah? Ebenezer? Emil?" Jupiter said.

"It's not nice to make fun of someone's name," Skinny fumed.

"Or maybe it's not a real name at all," Jupiter mused. "Maybe it's something like – like egret."

"All legs, and bony, with a big bill," Bob

said. "That works."

"Or elm," Pete said. "In other words, make like a tree and leave."

Skinny had turned beet-red and his hands were trembling. "You haven't heard the last of this!" he stammered.

"I think we have," Jupiter said. "Your friend just made a fool of you. Though I have observed that generally you need very little help."

Skinny looked as if he might explode. He turned, almost tripping over his own feet, and stalked back to the driver's side of his car. He opened the door, jumped in, revved the engine, revved it again for good measure, and put the car in reverse. When he stepped on the gas, he screeched backwards in an arc, so fast that he almost hit the side of the office.

Aunt Mathilda stuck her head out, looking aghast. "Good gracious!" she said.

Skinny put the car in drive and spun his wheels in his hurry to leave the Salvage Yard.

The coordinated counterattack they had mounted on Skinny had left them all feeling foolishly pleased with themselves, Bob thought. On the one hand, Skinny certainly deserved it. He was an example of how envy and jealousy could quickly get the best of you and twist you.

And the Three Investigators certainly had every reason to dislike him; he'd been a thorn in their side from the beginning.

Still, Bob thought, maybe their pleasure was a bit unseemly. After all, a victory over someone as puny as Skinny was not much to celebrate. And they had a case they should be focusing on. Even so, it took them a while to get back to it after they returned to the workshop and their chairs.

"Well, that was fun!" Pete said.

"And boy," Mallory said, "did Pete get it right about Skinny being jealous of Jupiter. One of Skinny's many problems is that he has absolutely no ambition. He thinks everything will be handed to him. You guys have worked for everything you have. It seems to drive him crazy."

"Thank you, Mallory," Jupiter said.

"So what was all that about?" Bob asked. "Do you think they'll really be calling the police?"

"I doubt it," Jupiter said. "Though I knew there was a possibility that my ploy with Ernie might backfire. I needed to look in a ledger that listed typewriter repairs, and I pretended to bribe him in order to get him to go away for a while."

"You know how good Jupiter is at lying," Pete said proudly. "Well, not really lying, but acting like someone else."

"Mallory and I were just talking about that, actually," Bob said. "Is it all right if I tell them what you said, Mallory?"

Mallory looked doubtful for a moment, but then nodded. "All right," she said.

"Mallory was saying that she's a good actor, too. A good liar, some might say. She was saying that since she's good at deceiving people when she wants to, she's also good at figuring out when other people are trying to do it, and she's really suspicious of Madhuri Singh."

Pete and Jupiter both gazed at Mallory with interest.

Pete said, "I'm not good at lying at *all*, and Bob really isn't either, but it's true that you were amazing that day with Daniel Hernández."

Jupiter nodded, then turned to Bob. "Before Skinny interrupted us, you were saying that Madhuri Singh grew up in Stratford-on-Avon," he said. "Pete and I found that out, too. Isabella Chang was invited to the Gala celebrating the reopening of the Theatre Festival's new building. Madhuri Singh was one of four people to give a brief speech. When she introduced Sir Iain she said she'd never had the chance to meet him in Stratford-on-Avon but had had to wait until he was appointed the artistic director of a theater in Rocky Beach."

"What!" exclaimed Bob. "Isabella Chang heard her say that?"

"That's what she said," Pete confirmed.

"That's pretty definitive," Mallory said. "Because Bob found an article in a London paper in which a man named Arjun Singh told the reporter he'd introduced his daughter Dhuri to Iain Anthony after he took her to a performance of *Macbeth*."

"Madhuri Singh's statement at the Gala would seem to be another lie, then," Jupiter said.

There was silence as they all considered this.

"There's one other thing," Jupiter added. "Isabella told us that when she was at the Gala, she had an odd experience when Sir Iain took the stage. She said she was frightened – that Sir Iain's face looked fierce and his voice sounded harsh. I keep feeling I should know what that reminds me of, but I don't. Does it ring any bells for you, Bob?"

"Not really," Bob answered. "Except

that Daman Duwalia also told us he was frightened. In his case, when the shanta murtis were switched for the raudra ones. But otherwise the two events don't have a lot in common."

"No, they don't," Jupiter acknowledged.

There was more silence, and then Bob took the conversation back to Madhuri Singh. "Her statement at the Gala is the second lie we know she's told," he said. "That dagger was new, not old. Has she told any other lies we know of?"

Jupiter pinched his lip and looked at Pete, then back at Bob and Mallory.

"Charlotte told us that Madhuri wanted to do *Macbeth* this summer, not *Romeo and Juliet*," he said, "and that conflicts with Madhuri's statement in the prop room that after she'd directed *Macbeth* as a student, she never tried her luck by directing the play again."

"Wow!" Bob said.

"Of course, a failed attempt to get permission to direct the play wouldn't, technically, contradict what she said," Jupiter added. "But although I was ready to believe that Sir Iain was responsible for what's been going on at the theater, Arjun Singh's story throws a new light on things. We're going to have to keep working to get to the bottom of all this."

Bob agreed. The news about the typewriter in Sir Iain's office had thrown him off balance. He'd come to the Salvage Yard that afternoon thinking Madhuri Singh was the prime suspect. Now he thought Sir Iain might be, after all.

"I guess we'll have another chance tomorrow night," Bob said.

"That's right," Jupiter said. He turned to Mallory. "Daman Duwalia has invited us to attend the play's technical rehearsal tomorrow night. Would you like to come with us? I'd find your input valuable."

"Yes," Mallory said, "I'd like that."

Bob could see that Mallory was keeping herself from looking as happy as she probably felt. She'd won Jupiter over − at least for the current case. The research Bob and Mallory had done that morning had been sufficient to give her a number of vantage points from which to look at what Jupiter would have called "the big picture." And yesterday she'd caught Madhuri Singh out in the lie about the dagger.

The fact was, Mallory's analyses were the sort that Jupiter himself made, and although Bob had noticed this some time ago, it seemed that Jupiter had finally noticed it, too.

9

The Blow From Heaven

When Pete got to the Salvage Yard the following evening, Bob, Jupiter, and Mallory were already there, waiting for him, and soon after, Worthington arrived to drive them up to the theater. Ever since Jupiter had brought up Isabella's story about her odd experience at the Gala, Pete had been thinking that he, too, had felt the same way at some time in his life, but even after trying hard to remember when it was or where he'd been or why he'd had those sorts of feelings, he simply couldn't, and as they wound their way through Rocky Beach, he shook his head to try to clear it and focus on the night ahead.

"Why is it called a technical rehearsal?" he asked anyone who would answer.

Glancing at him in the rear view mirror, Worthington said, "The director and cast will be running the play right from the beginning. But what they'll really be rehearsing are the technical aspects of the performance – sound effects, lighting changes, changes in the set, that sort of thing. They want to make sure the acting and the stagecraft work seamlessly."

"So they'll skip all the parts where the actors are just talking?" Pete asked.

"Exactly," Worthington said. "It can sometimes be a bit frustrating for them."

"But I heard Daman tell Jupiter they'll be doing the sword fights," Pete said.

"Yes," Worthington said. "I'm sure they will."

"I can't wait to see those," Pete said resolutely. He thought for a moment. "You know, Worthington, I think it's so cool that you studied fencing when you first got to Hollywood."

"Alas," Worthington said. "When they cast you as a chauffeur again and again, there's not much need for foils and épées."

"But you can do it," Bob said. "That's terrific in itself."

"I'm sure I'm more than a little rusty," Worthington said. "But as I mentioned earlier, I think it's something Jupiter would enjoy. It's a very cerebral sport, very much about strategy – about biding one's time and then seizing the opportunity."

"Maybe I'll try it," Jupiter said thoughtfully.

"You should, Jupe!" Pete exclaimed.

"You looked really good the other day when you picked up that rapier. Like a natural."

"I appreciate that," Jupiter said. "But right now I've got something else on my mind."

Pete knew what it was. Ever since Jupiter had learned that Sir Iain had a typewriter like the one the anonymous messages had come from, he'd wanted to get into Sir Iain's office to test it.

Worthington dropped them off by the main entrance. He told the boys he had several errands to run and would be back when he'd finished them. Pete and the others followed Jupiter. He'd arranged for the four of them to meet Daman Duwalia in his dressing room before the rehearsal began, and Daman was expecting them. He opened the door as soon as Jupiter knocked.

"Come in," he said.

With Mallory there, it was even more crowded tonight than it had been the other afternoon. Mallory seemed fascinated by the murtis and was asking Daman about Ganesha when Jupiter interrupted.

"I'm sorry, Mallory," he said, "but we need to fill Daman in on what we've discovered, and then I want to conduct my experiment." He turned to Daman who was standing by the door. "Were you aware that Madhuri Singh was a finalist for the job that Sir Iain got?" he asked.

"You mean the artistic directorship?" Daman asked, surprised. "No, I wasn't."

"Jupe and I went to typewriter repair shops yesterday and we found out that Reginald Ward – " Pete stopped when Jupiter held up his hand

"At the moment," Jupiter said, "the really important thing is that we discovered that Sir Iain has a typewriter in his office exactly like the one those anonymous messages were typed on. You said the other day that the various rooms and offices in the theater weren't locked, so I'm hoping we may be able to get into Sir Iain's office. I know it's the same model of typewriter, but we need to check the signature."

When Daman looked a bit confused, Jupiter reminded him what the word "signature" meant in this situation. "I need to type on the typewriter to see what the little quirks of his particular machine are. The typewriter we're looking for has "a"s and "e"s that float just above the line and "l"s that float just below it."

"You don't really think Sir Iain could have typed those letters?" Daman said.

"I'm sure he didn't!" Pete said vehemently. "It turns out that Reginald Ward took the typewriter into Shelley's Office Emporium just a month or so ago, and when he had it in his clutches, I bet he typed up the notes to try to scare you."

"I see," said Daman. "Though I still wouldn't have thought he had it in him."

"For now, we just need to see if the typewriter is a match," said Jupiter. "If it is, we can get into the arguments about who might have used it."

"O.K.," Daman said. "Follow me."

Jupiter was close on Daman's heels, and Pete and the others followed him down the hall and up another one. The office Daman took them to was much bigger than his dressing room − indeed, Pete thought, much bigger than any of the other offices. As they all saw at once, it had a lock, but the door was standing open. On either side of the door, the wall between the office and the hall was mostly glass, so if anyone came by while Jupiter was inside, they'd see him.

"I'm going in," Jupiter said. "You guys keep watch. If anyone comes, tell me, and I'll come back out."

"Be careful," Bob said.

"Be quick," Mallory said.

Pete was feeling a bit on edge. The other day at the typewriter place Jupiter's actions had been risky in one way, but this was risky in another. Pete was the lookout closest to Jupe, and he swiveled his head back and forth, between Jupiter and the hallway. His heartbeat picked up dramatically as he watched Jupiter calmly turn on the typewriter, insert a piece of paper into the roller, and begin typing. Pete watched as he typed something, then hit the return key and typed something else.

"Come on, come on," he muttered under his breath. But Jupiter kept typing. Again he hit the return key and typed some more, and again. "Jeez!" Pete whispered. "Hurry up!"

He was glad to see Jupiter turn off the typewriter, hurry through the door, and slip back into the hall. So was everyone else, it seemed. There was a collective sigh of relief.

"Come on," Jupiter said. "Let's see what we've got."

Back in Daman's dressing room, Jupiter said, "I'm sorry to have taken so long, but I needed to type "The quick brown fox jumped over the lazy dog" four times, twice in lowercase and twice in uppercase. Daman, could you hand me the originals of the letters you got?"

He went back and forth between the papers, examining closely. When he'd finished, he looked satisfied but also, it seemed to Pete, a little sad.

"I take no pleasure in announcing," said Jupiter, "that these are a perfect match. There's no question. These anonymous letters were typed on Sir Iain Anthony's typewriter."

"Let me see!" Pete said, and Jupiter handed him the pages. Bob and Mallory crowded around, all three of them looking closely. Pete could see Jupiter was right. The "a"s and "e"s Jupe had just typed rode slightly above the line.

"Wow!" he said.

"I still can't believe that Sir Iain would do such a thing," Daman said.

"Remember," Jupiter said. "All we're sure of is that the letters were typed on that machine. We still don't know who typed them."

"The truth of it is, almost anyone could have gotten in and used his typewriter," Bob said. "After all, Jupiter just did."

"That's true," Daman said.

"I still think it was Reginald Ward," Pete said. "After all, he's the one who took Sir Iain's typewriter in to be fixed."

"A possibility," Jupiter said. "We'll keep it firmly in mind. Pete, remind me to help you avoid jury duty if you're ever called to serve."

Bob and Mallory laughed. "What's so funny?" Pete asked.

"He means Reginald Ward is innocent until he's proven guilty," Bob said. "You can't jump to conclusions."

"When it comes to Reginald Ward, I can jump anywhere I want," Pete said. "He's friends with Skinny!"

"How much time do we have before you need to be on stage?" Jupiter asked.

Daman glanced at his watch. "About twenty minutes," he said. "Why?"

"I have a few questions I hope you can answer. I forgot to ask them at our last meeting."

Pete could see that Jupiter had gotten to that point in a case when all his energies were focused on it. He talked a bit more quickly, his actions were more clipped and decisive.

"Shoot," said Daman.

"I've heard you're not the first in your family to play Romeo," Jupiter said.

Daman smiled. "You mean my father?"

"Yes," Jupiter said. "Can you tell us anything about it?"

"There's not a lot to tell," Daman said. "When my parents were quite young, before they moved to America, they were cast in a Bollywood version of *Romeo and Juliet*. I've seen it, and it's kind of silly, with lots of dancing and sequins and stylized action. Also, it has a happy ending, like most Bollywood films. I thought my parents were pretty good, though."

"Do they have any enemies?" Jupiter asked. "Anyone who might wish to do them harm, by doing *you* harm?"

"Maybe an actor or actress who they beat out for the roles, or who was jealous of them?" Mallory asked.

Daman shook his head. "Not that I know of. I can ask them, I guess," he said.

"That would be good," Jupiter said. "I also meant to ask you if Madhuri Singh is married or in a relationship of some sort. I know she's not wearing a ring, but that's no sure guide these days."

Daman laughed. "Frankly, I don't know. I've never seen her with anyone. As far as I know she isn't, but she almost never says a word about her private life. I heard a rumor that she lives with someone, but then I've heard rumors about everyone and most of them are clearly made up. Anyway, if she *is* in a relationship, I don't think anyone has the faintest idea of who it is. The only thing I can tell you with any certainty is that she lives in Malibu." He glanced at his watch again. "I'd better be going," he added.

Pete and the others followed Daman down the hall and then backstage, which was now a bustle of actors and crew members. Everyone seemed very intent on getting things organized before the rehearsal began.

Pete, Jupiter, Bob, and Mallory left Daman backstage and made their way into the theater. Pete felt a little giddy from the combination of tension and excitement. It had been scary when Jupiter was in Sir Iain's office, but then again, he thought, if Jupiter had gotten caught, he'd have been sure to come up with a good excuse. At least that was behind them now – though he wished that Sir Iain hadn't been implicated. Pete had liked him very much. He had to try to remember that just because he liked someone, it didn't make them innocent.

As they sat in the theater, the house lights dimmed and the lights on stage came up. Madhuri Singh came striding from the wings. Almost immediately the racket of conversation on stage stopped. She looked taller than Pete knew she was. She radiated authority.

"Good evening, everyone," she said, smiling graciously. "It's tech night." She raised her hands as if to fend off their protestations. "I know, I know. Not anyone's favorite. Nevertheless, crucial. Billy, of course, will be helping me. Or I'll be helping him." She gestured to a blond guy in his thirties with wire-rimmed glasses who sat before a lectern in the orchestra pit. He had a big notebook in front of him, illuminated by a small light on the lecture.

"He's the stage manager," Mallory whispered. "He's in charge of cueing all the tech stuff."

"So we'll be moving pretty quickly," Madhuri Singh said. "You can save your beautiful rhetorical flourishes for the dress rehearsal. Tonight it's all about the stagecraft. So please bear with us. Either Billy or I will start the action and then stop it if we need to or want to. It's not even really important that you're fully in character. I just need your lines as cues so that we can make sure the computer's working when it needs to, and if there are any glitches — any at all — we'll go over it and over it until there aren't any. Questions?"

She looked around at the assemblage on stage. Pete noticed that Califia was standing next to Daman. He spotted Charlotte Mitchell in the back. Everyone on stage nodded.

The scene was an outdoor market, with wagons loaded with fruits and vegetables, and the play started with a prologue which surprised Pete by telling the whole story of the play, including the fact that Romeo and Juliet died in the end. Sort of a suspense killer, Pete thought.

There was a cue for a lighting change and two actors with swords and daggers entered. Not long after, two others joined them. It turned out the two pairs were from the two feuding families, and the swords came out. It was really fun to watch.

But too soon, as far as Pete was concerned, Madhuri Singh stopped the action. "O.K., O.K.," she called. "Good work, guys. Eddie, watch out that you don't turn your back on the audience. Let's move to the scene change."

Billy the stage manager turned around and pointed at a window in the back above the seats where a shadowy figure stood. Pete figured it must be the computer room. Sure enough, the wagons moved noiselessly into the wings, and a lamppost and a winding stone wall slipped on; the scene had been transformed into a street. "Wow!" Pete said.

He looked over at his friends. Each of them was studying the stage intently. Pete looked around the theater but Iain Anthony was nowhere to be seen.

The rehearsal moved pretty rapidly and, as far as Pete was concerned, quite jerkily. Just as he was getting into a scene, either Madhuri Singh or Billy ended it. Sometimes they went back over a scene change or a lighting cue. But for the most part, everything seemed to be working pretty well. Pete was more and more excited to see the whole play without anything being left out.

They were at the beginning of Act III when there was a great crashing noise and a cry from the wings at the right of the stage. Everything stopped; there were some voices raised, and Pete could see concern on the faces of some of the actors.

Madhuri Singh hobbled into view, favoring her right leg. She waved her hands and was laughing. "It's nothing, it's nothing," she said. "So sorry for the interruption. Let's go on. Don't mind me."

"What happened?" one of the actors close to her asked.

"I tripped over something in the wings, and almost fell flat on my face," she said. "I could have sworn it wasn't there the moment before, but – well – things don't move by themselves, so I just must not have been keeping track. Has anyone seen my good luck dagger? It seems to have gone missing."

The actors and crew members turned to one another, confused, and started talking.

"No?" Madhuri Singh said. "Well, give it to me if it turns up. I've had it for twenty years, ever since I directed 'the Scottish play,' and – "

She started laughing. "I was going to say it hasn't failed me yet, but come to think of it, it hasn't been doing a very good job recently. Actually, I almost wish this *were* the Scottish play. I can't imagine having as much bad luck on that as I've had on this one. A sprained ankle, a cut face, and now this." She laughed again. "Either that or I'm getting mighty clumsy in my old age."

Pete saw she was trying to seem upbeat, but why was she reminding everyone of this? He could sense a feeling of unease spread among the actors on stage. Daman looked alarmed, and Pete felt his own pulse pick up.

Things settled down a bit as they ran the next scene until Madhuri stopped the action to say that one of the spots was all wrong and needed to be adjusted. She glanced around, but the crew member she was looking for was nowhere to be found.

"Reggie," she said to Reginald Ward. "Be a dear and get up on the catwalk and fix the spot, will you?"

At the mention of Reginald Ward's name, Pete sat up very straight.

"But I'm not − I mean why would I − ," Reginald Ward blustered.

"Romeo just killed you in a street brawl," Madhuri Singh said. "So you can spare the time. Please?"

Ward wasn't happy about it but he complied. He disappeared into the wings, and Pete imagined he was climbing a ladder up to the catwalks that crossed the stage high up, out of view of the audience.

He still hadn't quite shaken the shock of Madhuri Singh's interruption. She seemed to have suggested that someone had intentionally moved whatever she had tripped over so that she would hurt herself. If that were true, then the culprit was right there on stage. Pete looked from one actor to the other with a mounting sense of apprehension. Or had it been Reginald Ward himself?

So he was already feeling quite tense

when the feeling of apprehension crept over him, as though someone were watching him from behind. He whirled around and surveyed the back of the theater but there was no one there. His neck prickled as he turned back to the stage.

He could feel his heart begin to beat more quickly. He glanced at his friends. Bob was shifting in his seat uncomfortably as though he felt it too. A hollow pit was beginning to form in Pete's stomach, and his breathing had become more shallow. There was no reason for him to be afraid, but he was.

On stage Romeo had fled in despair to the cell of Friar Lawrence, who had earlier married him and Juliet. After Romeo had killed Juliet's brother Tybalt in a fight, the prince of Verona had banished him, and he thought that being separated from Juliet was as bad as death.

"Stop!" Madhuri Singh said. "I want that spot on Romeo now."

Almost like magic a beam of light fell from above, illuminating Daman Duwalia.

"Watch your mark," Madhuri Singh said, gesturing to the stage, and Daman looked down and adjusted his position slightly. He had both a rapier and a dagger in his belt.

"Now," Madhuri Singh said. She pushed Daman gently out of the way and stood under the spotlight herself. She was illuminated brilliantly – her dark hair, her bright eyes, the glint of diamond in her left nostril.

"Listen to these lines," she said, and she recited Romeo's part by heart:

There is no world without Verona walls,
But purgatory, torture, hell itself.
Hence-banished is banished from the world,
And world's exile is *death* –

She paused on the last word. Pete had felt all twisted up inside like this before, he thought, as though he were in imminent danger, but he couldn't put his finger on when. Out of the blue a feeling of nervousness had blossomed in his chest and had grown and grown until – .

On stage, Madhuri Singh was still declaiming. "That's where Romeo and Juliet are headed, of course," she said dramatically. "Straight for the tomb. Exiled from the world. But at the moment, Romeo thinks mere banishment is bad. Ha ha! He'll soon find out it isn't. All of you, every one of you – but especially Daman and Califia – needs to open yourselves completely – " She flung her arms wide " – to the idea of *death*."

The word *death* seemed to reverberate through the theater as if it had been amplified. Then everything was silent for a second, and in the silence Pete heard what sounded like a faint clack. Several members of the cast looked up and screamed but Madhuri Singh stood rooted to the floor as something glinting in the light flashed very close by her, whistling, and stuck with a big thunk into the stage. It was like a blow from heaven hitting earth.

Pete yelled and leaped to his feet. He was close enough to the stage to see what it was that had hit the floorboards. As it had fallen, it had just missed Madhuri Singh, but there, gleaming in the spotlight and quivering from its sudden impact with the stage floor, was Madhuri's good luck dagger.

10

A Dangerous Game

Chaos ensued. Jupiter, too, jumped to his feet, shocked by the suddenness of what had just happened. The stage lighting came full on, flooding the place with white light. In its glare, Madhuri Singh stood stock-still, staring at the spot, not more than two feet from her, where the dagger stuck in the wood.

Next to Jupiter, Pete was pointing and talking fast. "Holy moly!" he said. "Where did that come from? It was almost like – ." To Jupiter it seemed as though Pete was having a bit of trouble taking a deep breath. "And did you have it, too?" he finally spit out. "That spooky nervous feeling Isabella Chang was talking about?"

"Yes," Jupiter said. "But it seems to have stopped now."

Pete looked at Jupiter, amazed. "You're right!" he said. He patted himself down with his hands as if looking for something under his clothes.

On stage, Califia emerged from the wings and hurried up to Madhuri. In the hulla-

187

baloo, Jupiter could hear nothing, but from the expression on her face, he knew Califia must be asking if Madhuri Singh was O.K. She had put her hand on the older woman's back.

"Califia looks so calm," Pete said. "I'm not calm at all, and I wasn't even up on stage! Her director was almost killed right in front of her eyes and she's just dealing with it."

Jupiter watched as Califia came to the stage's apron, shaded her eyes from the bright lights, and peered out into the audience. In no time, she had left the stage, come out the door and down the steps, and hurried over to them.

"Wow!" Pete said. "I can't believe what just happened. And you're so calm!"

"I may look calm," Califia said. "But I'm really not. I guess I'm just acting calm."

"Well, you're doing a good job," Bob said. "You fooled me."

"What's going to happen now?" Pete asked. "Do you have any idea where that dagger came from? Some good luck charm!"

"Somewhere above the stage," Califia said. "Up on the catwalk or higher, up in the fly."

"How could the dagger have gotten up there?"

"I don't know," Califia said.

"It came so close!" Pete said. "It was like it was headed straight for her. As if it was trying to get her."

"Excuse me," Jupiter said.

There was no direct access to the stage from the orchestra pit, so he went around to the back, then through the wings. By the time he got to the stage, the actors had crowded around Madhuri Singh.

"We ought to call the police!" one of them said.

"No, no," Madhuri Singh said. "Let's not be hasty. Let's think this through. I'm fine – a little shaken, perhaps, but fine. We have to think of the theater first, of course, and of Sir Iain. That old saying about how there's no such thing as bad publicity – well, that's just not true. And things are already a little shaky, aren't they? First, the Gala was such a flop, and now there are so many unfortunate whispers about how Sir Iain is, well – "

"Losing it?" someone said.

Madhuri Singh looked stern. "Now, I didn't say that," she said emphatically. "But people will gossip. I've even heard rumors – I'm sure you've all heard them -- that what Sir Iain is suffering from isn't Parkinson's at all, but some little-known form of dementia."

She shook her head, looking puzzled at the vicious nature of her fellow creatures. "People can be so cruel."

"I still think we should call the police," the actor repeated. "Someone tried to kill you."

Madhuri Singh looked doubtful. "Me?" she said. "Why would someone want to kill me? The person who should have been standing where I was standing was Daman Duwalia." She looked up at Daman, who took a step backward in surprise. Jupiter could see that the thought had not occurred to him before.

"But why would anyone want to harm either of us?" Madhuri Singh went on. "I'm sure there's a perfectly logical explanation. In fact, it may very well have been my own fault."

"What do you mean?" Daman asked.

"Quite simply that I may have had my lucky charm with me a couple days ago when I went up onto the catwalk to check on the housing of one of the spots. In my frazzled state, I probably just put the dagger down; you'll remember I said I couldn't find it. So it could have just dropped," she said. "Or maybe when I sent Reggie up to fix that spot, the vibrations nudged it closer to the edge."

An ingenious explanation, Jupiter thought. And it might actually be true.

"Don't blame me!" Reginald Ward said hotly to the assemblage. "I didn't do anything! I just went up there because Madhuri asked me to. You heard her." He looked around like a cornered animal. "And I couldn't have knocked it down or dropped it because I was still up there when it fell right past me. It could have killed *me!*" He smacked his chest with both fists, deeply aggrieved. "I wasn't trying to hurt anyone."

"Of course not," Madhuri Singh said. "No one alive would think such a thing."

That wasn't true, Jupiter thought. He could think of one person – Pete – who would certainly think it.

"Besides," Madhuri Singh said. "Nothing really happened, did it? I tripped, a dagger fell from the sky – " She looked up, gesturing, and everyone laughed.

"And why should we draw attention to what some might see as a lapse in security on Sir Iain's part? Besides, if the Rocky Beach police are summoned, there'll undoubtedly be some breathless and inaccurate news article in the paper, and, if that happens, there will almost certainly be no opening night for our production."

Jupiter could see that no one on stage

wanted that to happen.

Madhuri Singh stood and looked around her. "No," she said. "Let's leave things be. But I think I ought to get that dagger out of here so it doesn't keep reminding us – "

"No," one of the actors said. "Even if we don't call the police, that dagger's an important piece of evidence. Maybe later it could be checked for fingerprints."

Madhuri Singh smiled gratefully. "You're so right," she said. "Could someone get a pair of latex gloves and a plastic bag?"

Jupiter found himself thinking about what had happened in the moments before the dagger had fallen. When he thought back on it, it was almost as though the process had been speeded up. He saw again the spotlight coming on, how the figure of Daman Duwalia had leapt out at him in the scalding whiteness, how Madhuri Singh had jostled him out of position as if to take possession of the spot, how she had gestured and exclaimed and how the dagger had fallen just after she said the word *death*.

It had been hard to comprehend because, at the same time it was happening, Jupiter's skin had begun to creep and he'd been filled with nameless dread. He knew something like this had happened to him before, but when? It was like a name on the tip of his tongue that he just could not recall.

By now, Jupiter had been joined by Mallory and Califia and Pete and Bob. As someone went to get the glove and plastic bag to protect the evidence, Madhuri Singh crossed her arms on her chest and looked around her benevolently.

"This has been a great strain on all of you," she said. "But we have almost half a play to finish. Why don't we take a break and reconvene in, say, thirty minutes?"

Ever since he'd arrived on stage Pete had been staring upwards. Now he looked at Jupiter and spoke in a harsh whisper.

"Jupe!" he said. "Reginald Ward was lying! He said that knife fell right past him, but there's nothing up there above the catwalks. Just the roof and some lights! That's it! You'd have to be a bat or a bird to have dropped the dagger from up there."

"Yes," Jupiter said. "It will take some puzzling through."

Pete went back to staring at the ceiling while Jupiter studied the dagger. Fully an inch of its eight-inch blade had dug into the wood of the stage. He remembered the surprise he'd felt when he first saw the knife and the further surprise he'd felt when he'd discovered it was magnetized. As swiftly as he could, he took out his Swiss Army knife, knelt on the stage floor, leaned forward, and touched his blade to the dagger's blade.

Before he was an inch away, he felt the force pull his knife in. He pulled it loose and let it be pulled in again. The dagger was still magnetized. In fact, if anything, the charge it held was stronger than it had been that day in the prop room. He looked around him at the stage floor. There were several crosses made of blue tape which he assumed had been placed in specific spots so actors would know exactly where to stand for a lighting effect or other bit of stagecraft to work. One of the marks was just a few feet from where the dagger stood upright. He looked more closely at the stage. About an inch from where the blade had stabbed the wood, he saw another stab wound.

The break in the rehearsal was a stroke of luck, Jupiter thought. His mind was whirring, as he put together Reginald Ward's assertion with what he'd just discovered. So many people had left the stage that he was quite unhindered when he went to the ladder leading to the catwalks and started to climb up. As he got higher and higher above the stage floor, he had a slightly queasy feeling in his stomach. He wasn't fond of heights, especially when all he had around him were a few metal bars. He climbed up onto the catwalk and inched his way along until he was almost directly above the dagger, which was still stuck in the stage.

The queasy feeling brought him back to those moments before the dagger fell, when he and Pete – and presumably Bob and Mallory, though he hadn't asked them yet – had been engulfed for no apparent reason in a fog of fear. It was almost like – yes, it was!

He was happy to finally remember the other time this had happened, and he lay down on the catwalk, put his arms at his sides, and took a few deep breaths. Remembering seemed to have cleared his head quite dramatically, and Jupiter studied the ceiling of the theater, studded with can lights. Directly over the dagger – though not directly over Jupiter – was a light surrounded by a wide metal rim that looked like steel.

Jupiter stared. It would be theoretically possible, he thought, to have placed an electromagnet under the steel rim of the can light, and also theoretically possible to have placed the dagger up against it. If the electromagnet was on, the weapon would have been magnetized by the charge and would also have been held fast against the plate. That is, until the moment the electromagnet was shut off. At that point, the dagger, with its weighted blade, would have dropped straight down until it stabbed the floor – or the top of anyone's head who had happened to get in the way. This was a dangerous game someone was playing.

He smiled grimly. Quite clever, he thought. Fiendishly clever. And whoever had done this had tested the process in advance. That was the reason he'd found an identical stab wound in the wood not more than an inch from where the blade now stuck. It had been engineered quite perfectly. He felt sure that if the dagger were attached again to the electro-magnet and allowed again to fall, a tight little locus of stab wounds would occur.

So someone had "practiced" in secret what had happened tonight in plain view. That would explain why the dagger had been mag-netized when Pete's rapier had touched it in the prop room.

Below Jupiter a commotion was taking place. He looked down to see Sir Iain walking quickly across the stage. Almost like magic, members of the cast and crew re-materialized. Jupiter got to his feet, inched along the catwalk, and then clambered down the ladder as quickly as he could. Califia, Bob, Pete, and Mallory were now back onstage as well. They had been joined by Daman, and Jupiter gathered from the overlapping conversations that Sir Iain had been in his office and someone had alerted him to what had happened.

Though Sir Iain was clearly upset, he was calm and reassuring to all around him. He said quite forcefully that the police should be called, but he didn't pull rank and he listened carefully to the competing arguments. He seemed to Jupiter eminently sane and rational, and his voice was deep, sonorous, and reassuring – the opposite of a voice that would agitate or unnerve.

Above all, he seemed sure of himself, comfortable in his skin, and fully *there* in a way that argued strongly against the possibility of dementia.

It seemed that Sir Iain was unconvinced by the competing arguments until Madhuri Singh stepped in.

"My dear," Sir Iain said, clearly not having noticed her before. "Are you quite all right?"

"Yes, Iain, thank you," she said. "And I agree that this is a serious matter. But as I was saying before to the cast and crew, nothing really happened in the end, and when I think about the damage that this incident, if reported, could do to the reputation of this theater and to this production – ”

“That may be true,” Sir Iain said. “But at times like this, we must think of the bigger picture.”

Members of the cast clambered for his attention, repeating Madhuri Singh’s arguments. They began wheedling and whining, until Madhuri stepped in again.

“Perhaps this might be a compromise, Sir Iain. Why don’t you take the dagger and lock it in the safe in your office until after opening night? Once we’re past that, I don’t think the story will hurt us or the theater much. It’s just a short delay and you’ll be protecting the only evidence there is.”

“All right,” Sir Iain said, “since all of you seem of a single mind. But I urge you to write down everything you can remember about the rehearsal when you get home tonight – paying particular attention to the time just before and after the dagger fell. That will help the police when they do get around to asking questions.”

Jupiter was impressed by this sound advice. He watched as a stagehand, wearing latex gloves, carefully rocked the dagger's blade until he could easily pull it from the wood. He slipped it into a plastic bag and presented it rather formally to Sir Iain, who took it and nodded gracefully.

"Madhuri, why don't you come with me?" he said.

Jupiter looked to the others, and then he, Pete, Mallory, Daman, Bob, and Califia followed Sir Iain and Madhuri. Jupiter stood in the doorway, the others clustered around him. Through the glass they watched as Sir Iain opened his safe, slipped the dagger in, closed the door, and twirled the lock.

"There," he said. "It'll be safe now. And no one can pick this lock; it's electromagnetic. You've certainly had a run of bad luck, my dear," he said, kindly putting his hand on Madhuri's shoulder. "But I'm sure it's over now. I must say I'm glad, however, that I didn't accede to your request to direct – " He lowered his voice to a stage whisper. " – the Scottish play!" He chuckled and walked with her toward the door.

This was Jupiter's signal to leave, and he suggested that the six of them retire to Daman's dressing room for a debriefing. It was a tight fit. There was some friendly jostling until everyone found a place – on a chair, the low table, or the dressing table.

Once everyone was seated, Jupiter explained his hypothesis about an electromagnet inside the can light, but although everyone seemed impressed, and convinced by the logic of the suggestion, they all said they couldn't quite imagine either Reginald Ward *or* Sir Iain coming up with such a scheme.

"I understand your reservations," Jupiter said, "but we must remember that Sir Iain has spent his whole life in the theater or on film sets, and by now he knows a whole lot about special effects. At the same time, I cannot see what Sir Iain's motive might have been. And he certainly doesn't seem ill in any way."

Jupiter paused and looked at the others closely. "Let me ask you something else," he said. "In the run-up to the dagger falling, I experienced some strange sensations. I know Pete did as well, but I don't know about the rest of you. Did any of you feel unnaturally nervous or fearful or anxious?" They all looked a little surprised and told him that yes, they had.

"But things were getting so extreme," Califia said, "with that speech Madhuri made."

"Granted," Jupiter said, nodding. "Daman, was what you felt this evening anything like the feeling you had the morning you discovered the murtis had been switched?"

Daman looked astounded. "Now that I think about it, yes," he said. "Exactly like that – though it was less powerful tonight."

"Ever since it happened I've been analyzing it," Jupiter said, "and I've come to the conclusion that it was not natural. For one thing, why would all of us have been feeling the same thing at the same time? Also, the other day a friend of ours who attended the Gala at the start of the theater season described similar feelings she'd had that night, and this evening I finally remembered what her description reminded me of."

He turned to Pete and Bob. "You felt it too. Remember a time when a feeling of unease turned into extreme nervousness and went straight to – well – terror?"

"Terror Castle!" Pete said, jumping to his feet. "Of course!"

"Why didn't I think of that?" Bob said.

"I can only assume that what caused us to feel those feelings at Terror Castle must be causing them here," Jupiter said. "Not a pipe organ, of course, but something that produces vibrations below the range of human hearing and that consequently causes irrational feelings of distress and fear."

"Subsonic sounds?" asked Mallory.

"Exactly," said Jupiter. "Although they're calling them infrasonic now. Either way, they could be piped though a sophisticated sound system."

"But that's not something Sir Iain would know how to do, "Pete said. "And why would he want to make people feel afraid when he was speaking at his own Gala? All right, maybe tonight, if he was trying to scare Madhuri Singh or Daman. But Isabella Chang said the feeling didn't begin on the night of the Gala until Sir Iain started speaking. It *must* have been Reginald Ward."

Jupiter pinched his bottom lip. What Pete was saying had a lot of truth to it. But was Reginald Ward smart enough to have come up with a scheme like this? And if Reginald really had been involved, then had his target actually been Daman, or did he have some grudge against Madhuri Singh? Or could Sir Iain Anthony really have an unusual form of dementia? After all, he would have had the power and influence to organize a plot like this and could even have convinced his son's wife's nephew to help him.

In that scenario, Reginald Ward was no

mastermind but just an underling — a role he was much better suited for. But why would Sir Iain have wanted to hurt either Daman Duwalia *or* Madhuri Singh? And who had actually arranged for infrasonic sounds to be piped into the theater and Daman's dressing room? Presumably the same person who had placed the electromagnet behind the can light — but who *was* that, exactly? Jupiter wondered.

"We'd better get on stage," Daman said to Califia. "It's been about a half hour. Thank you guys for all you're doing. I hope you can figure this out, because it makes my head hurt."

"Yes," Califia said. "Great to see you all. I'm sorry tonight was such a bust, but I do hope you'll all come to the dress rehearsal. And bring your parents, if you can."

Then Daman and Califia were gone, and Jupiter and his friends got ready to follow. Jupiter noticed the sample page he'd typed on Sir Iain's typewriter. He picked it up and handed it to Bob.

"This is for you, Records," he said, "to keep with the copies of Daman's letters. I wish we could get a copy of a document typed by Sir Iain himself. It's possible the typing might be different under different people's fingers. It would be easy enough to ask Charlotte to get us something Sir Iain had typed – particularly if I told her we were trying to clear his name. But that might lead to Sir Iain learning about our suspicions. It's a quandary."

"You'll think of something, Jupe," Pete said. "You always do."

Jupiter smiled. Pete's faith in him was unbounded. He hoped that the day never came when he would let Pete down. But as they walked out of the theater to look for Worthington and the Flex, Jupiter was worried that day might come sooner than later. He was feeling pretty uncomfortable with the way things were going. He had a lot of suspicions and had reached a number of unassailable conclusions. But they were based in logic and not in proof. He was afraid this might be the very first case The Three Investigators never fully solved.

That would be bad in itself, but after tonight the odds also seemed high that, at the end of the summer season, if not before, Sir Iain Anthony would be forced out of his job as the artistic director of the Rocky Beach Summer Theater Festival. Which would be all well and good if Sir Iain were responsible for these events. But it would be *very* unfair if he wasn't.

11

An Interesting Hypothesis

The next morning, Bob found his father sitting at the round glass table on the patio outside the kitchen of their house, lingering over a second cup of coffee. Bob's mother had already left for another committee meeting at Reedmore College. Bob had brought a bowl of cereal out with him, and he ate while sparrows chattered in the trees above them. Despite the upset of last night, he was feeling pretty good this morning.

"I'm glad you're still here, Dad," Bob said. "I was hoping to talk to you about something."

The night before, on the way back from the theater, Jupiter had told everyone he needed a day off to think, and Pete had said that his father wanted help with a new deck he was building on their house, so even though Bob was due to work in the library that afternoon, he had the morning off. He was planning to bicycle over to Mallory's apartment and spend a couple of hours with Mallory and Califia; Mallory had invited Bob to join them, and he had accepted.

Now, Bob's father put down the paper he was reading, took off his glasses, and rubbed his eyes.

"So," he asked, "have you cracked the theater case yet?"

"Not yet," Bob said. "Usually by now we know who we're after. But not this time. Too many suspects." He explained what had happened at the technical rehearsal, described the rumors swirling around Sir Iain, and told his father what Madhuri Singh had said about him.

"I don't know what to think," he added. "When I met Sir Iain at the theater, he seemed like a really great guy, and last night when he took charge of the situation, he acted quite sensibly. But the rumors make him sound sinister – really scary."

"It's funny you should say that," his father said. "While you boys were up in Auburn, your mother and I were invited to the Theatre Festival's re-opening Gala. I'm sure they hoped I'd write an article they could use for publicity purposes. In fact, I intended to, but what happened was so bizarre I didn't."

Bob hadn't known his parents had gone to the Gala, and he was stunned – in a good way — to guess that his father had had the same experience Isabella Chang had had. He stared at him for a moment, then smiled.

"You mean," he said, "that when Sir Iain started giving his speech you began to feel uneasy, and then more and more anxious, until you finally wanted to run right out of the theater?"

"How on earth did you know that?" Mr. Andrews asked, putting his glasses back on and staring at his son.

Bob paused for a moment, enjoying his father's reaction. Then he explained.

"The same thing happened to Isabella Chang," he said. "She's a long-time patron of the theater. Not only that, but something similar happened to us at the tech rehearsal last night. Jupiter thinks it's subsonic sound that's creating these feelings without people even knowing where they're coming from. Like the pipe organ in the Terror Castle case."

"Ah, yes," Bob's father said. "I remember that. If that's what's going on, then it sounds as though someone is hard at work trying to ruin Sir Iain Anthony's reputation."

"I basically agree," Bob said. "But there's some evidence against him, as well. Jupiter proved last night that those anonymous letters Daman Duwalia got were typed on the typewriter in Sir Iain's office. The trouble is, we don't know if they were typed by Sir Iain or by someone else. We'd like to get our hands on something Sir Iain actually typed."

"I think I can help you there," his father said. He left the table, went inside, and returned with a fancy cream-colored card embossed on the front with an I and an A intertwined. He opened it and set it down in front of Bob.

"It's a note from Sir Iain. I received it a week after the Gala. I assume he sent thank-you notes to all the journalists and important donors who'd attended."

"Wow!" Bob said, lifting it up to read it. The card was thick and expensive-looking, and he studied the message carefully – comparing it in his mind to the page Jupiter had given him for safekeeping.

"I'll be right back," he told his father. He ran upstairs to his room and returned with the paper.

"This is the sheet Jupiter typed on the typewriter last night," he said.

His father examined the note and the sample typing side by side. "Markedly different," he said. "Look at the cross-outs and typed-over letters in the note from Sir Iain."

"And a lot of the letters are very faint," Bob said. "I suppose you'd have a hard time typing with Parkinson's. Can I keep this for a while?" he asked his father. "To show Jupiter?"

"That'll be fine," his father said. "Now didn't you tell me you were going to spend the morning with two young women? When are you supposed to get there?"

"Gosh!" Bob said. "You're right! I don't want to be late!"

He rushed to his room and stuffed his computer and the paper into his backpack. Then he jumped on his bike and was off to the Wessex House. He'd woken up feeling good, and now he felt even better. He was glad he'd be able to give Jupiter the note from Sir Iain, but even more glad to have been invited to Mallory's. There, he leaned his bike against the porch, climbed the steps, and walked briskly down the hall to her apartment.

She opened the door just moments after he knocked. She looked happy to see him, and even if she *didn't* like him except as a friend, Bob thought, he was still glad she'd moved to Rocky Beach. She was wearing the kilt-like shorts she'd worn the first time she'd biked by the Salvage Yard.

"Hi," she said. "Califia's already here."

The sun had not gotten around to the south, so it wasn't yet pouring in the living room windows as it had the last time Bob had been there. Otherwise the living room was comfortably familiar. The sheer curtains over the windows made the outside world look pleasantly gauzy and indistinct; the pots that held the ferns, ivy, and banana tree gave off the smell of freshly watered earth. The forest-green velvet sofa glowed and, in the middle of it, Califia sat drinking a cup of coffee. She was wearing shorts and sandals and a white cropped top. For years, Bob had been a bit intimidated by her extroverted ways and her ability as a public speaker, but during the last few days, he'd gotten more comfortable being around her.

"Hi, Bob," Califia said. "Mallory just showed me the trunk you guys had made for her. It's really beautiful."

"I'm glad you like it," he said. "Leif and Magnus made it and an artist friend of theirs painted it. I thought it turned out great."

Bob noticed that Mallory's antique Scottish dagger with the banded silver scabbard lay on the coffee table. Mallory had inherited it from her father, and when Califia saw that

Bob had noticed it, she said, "Mallory was showing me that, too, and we were wondering why Madhuri said her dagger was twenty years old. I just can't see why she'd lie about it."

"Would you like some coffee?" Mallory asked Bob. When he shook his head, she said, "I've been trying to convince Califia that Jupiter was right when he said that people lie to protect themselves, cover their reputations, or fool other people into doing or thinking things they otherwise wouldn't do or think. Maybe you can help me."

Mallory sat down next to Califia on the sofa, and when Bob had settled himself in a nearby chair, Mallory went on with her explanation.

"Understandably, Califia doesn't want to believe anything bad about Madhuri Singh, and I *still* haven't been able to come up with an actual, concrete reason why she would have lied about having a so-called 'good luck dagger'. But there has to be one. And it may have something to do with protecting her reputation."

Bob thought for a moment. "I've always believed ambition was something only certain people − like Sir Iain − had, but it's really something everyone is born with. Even us.

Califia wants to be a really good actress, and I'd like to get better as a writer. It made me happy when Daman told me he liked my writing."

"So you think Madhuri Singh is really ambitious?" asked Califia. "I can't see that."

"But she went to great lengths to press the point that Sir Iain might have something wrong with his brain," Mallory said. "Why did she do that, if not to place suspicion on him and deflect it from herself? Bob, did you see any evidence last night that Sir Iain isn't of sound mind?"

"No," Bob said. "He seemed like the sanest guy around. And take a look at this!" He pulled out the sheet Jupiter had typed and the note his father had gotten from Sir Iain. Both Mallory and Califia were quick to notice the differences.

"So we now know that Sir Iain didn't type the anonymous notes," Mallory said. "And we know that someone has gone to a lot of trouble with the subsonic rumbling and the dagger. I was really impressed with Jupiter's theory of how they got the dagger to fall. But I can't understand why he would still consider Sir Iain a suspect – in cahoots with some technical wizard. I thought before last night that Madhuri Singh was the obvious suspect, and what happened at the theater just confirmed my suspicions. All of her 'accidents' and the threatening letters she's supposedly received are misdirection."

"Also, Charlotte Mitchell – who I trust – works for Sir Iain part-time and insists he's a totally great guy," Bob said.

"You see?" Mallory said to Califia.

"You may be right," Califia said. "But I still think there's something a little strange about the man."

"I've never met him in person, so I can't say," said Mallory. "And I do have to admit that even though I think she's guilty, I can't figure out what Madhuri Singh might have against Daman – ."

"Exactly," Califia said triumphantly.

This was a very slippery case, Bob thought. Where were the motives? Just when he had crossed someone off the suspect list, one of his friends came up with a good reason to put them back on. Granted, he hadn't seen anything "strange" about Sir Iain, but Califia had seen a whole lot more of him than he had.

Califia was insistent. "And if you think it was Madhuri," she said, "then why was she almost killed last night?"

"That's another thing that seems hard to explain," Mallory admitted. "Although if she hadn't pushed Daman out of the way, it might have been him."

"Oh my gosh," Califia said. "I don't want to think that someone might really be trying to hurt him. He's so great – to work with and all." She blushed faintly. "Someone that famous could just stay in his dressing room or leave the theater entirely except when he's on stage. But he's always around, and so friendly to everyone."

"It sounds like you've spent a lot of time with him," Bob said, smiling.

"It's hard to avoid when you're playing Romeo and Juliet," Califia said. "I've told him a lot about my life and he's told me about his. Just the other day he was talking about his parents and about how great he thinks it is that they're still in love with one another after all these years. He said if he ever got married he wanted to have a marriage as good as theirs."

"The two of you are talking about marriage?" Mallory said incredulously.

"Just in general terms!" Califia said and then started laughing – the kind of giddy laughter that Bob knew stemmed from embarrassment.

"I told Mallory this already," she added, "but I have a sort of crush on Daman. Madhuri was being all motherly, telling me she didn't want to see me get hurt. That when the play was over he'd go back to L.A. and his work on films. Of course I know that. It's not like I think this could turn into some long-term thing. It's just exciting to meet a new person."

Bob thought they were losing the thread of the mystery a bit, but they hadn't really been scheduled to discuss the mystery, anyway. Since Califia clearly wanted to share her experience with Mallory, he thought the least he could do was be quiet and listen. Califia went on to say that her parents had met in college when they were off on their own, while Daman's parents had met all the way back in high school. At the time they were still living with their parents. In India. And then, to Bob's surprise, Califia started talking about arranged marriages.

"Did you know that ninety percent of marriages in India are still arranged?" Califia said.

"That's incredible," Mallory said. "I'd say it was horrible, except that I've read that in certain countries arranged marriages actually have a very high success rate."

"Really?" Califia asked, amazed. "Anyway, both of Daman's parents were supposed to marry people their parents picked for them. Daman's father was engaged to a girl he'd never met, whose parents had immigrated to England. She sent him pictures and wrote him letters and just did the whole getting-to-know-you thing long distance. Daman said Indian immigrants in the U.K. still have lots of strong ties with family and friends back in India."

A little tickle of puzzlement was starting in the back of Bob's mind. How old was Daman's father now? he wondered. Mallory had an expression on her face that was hard to decipher – she was clearly thinking hard.

"It's such a romantic story," Califia said. "When Daman's parents fell in love, right away they resolved not to marry the people their parents had picked out for them. Daman's father rebelled first. Both his parents came from well-known families, so the tabloids got hold of it and splashed it across the front pages. 'Children Fall in Love and Disobey Parents.' Just like in *Romeo and Juliet.*"

Califia smiled and stretched her legs out onto the table next to the dagger.

"The scandal got so big and went on for

so long that a famous Bollywood director thought it would be a great publicity stunt to do a Bollywood version of *Romeo and Juliet* and cast Daman's parents in the roles," Califia went on. "So that's how they got their start as actors! Isn't that cool? Of course, it wouldn't be a good story if Daman's parents hadn't turned out to be so talented and to have had such brilliant careers. Not to mention a son like Daman."

"It's a remarkable story," Mallory said with what seemed to Bob suppressed excitement. "Do you have any idea what happened to the girl Daman's father decided not to marry?"

"No," Califia said. "Why?"

"Because she was probably pretty upset, don't you think?" Mallory said.

"Yeah, she probably was," Califia said, her face falling. "Poor girl. How awful. I hadn't thought of that."

"You wouldn't know what the girl's name was, would you?" Mallory asked, and when she said this, Bob finally understood what the tickle of puzzlement had been.

He was impressed by how quickly Mallory had connected the two stories — one about an Indian girl who had grown up in England,

and the other about a man who had once been engaged to marry such a girl. That connection made sense, but it was also a daring leap from one thing to another.

"No," Califia said. "Why would I?"

Mallory looked at her half in admiration and half in exasperation. What Madhuri Singh had said about Califia's innocence had been spot on, Bob thought. Although she and Pete were, in some ways, very different, at the moment Califia's innocence reminded him of Pete's.

Since Mallory clearly didn't want to say what had to be said,   Bob said, as gently as possible, "I think Mallory is suggesting that the girl might have been Madhuri Singh."

The look on Califia's face told Bob that she would not have considered this possibility in a billion years. She looked thunderstruck.

"What?" she said. "You think Madhuri Singh and Daman Duwalia's father might have been engaged?"

"Think of it this way," Mallory said. "Before, I said that I couldn't think of any reason Madhuri Singh might have for wanting to hurt Daman. Now I can."

Bob could, too. The whole time Califia had been talking, he'd been thinking about how the girl back in England must have felt. Daman's father's parents had probably been upset, but not as upset as the girl would have been. She'd been going along, doing what she was told to do, dreaming of a happy life with a particular man, and then whammo! It was over. It might make someone angry, angry enough – ”

“No,” Califia said. “I don't believe it! At least – well – I –. Do you mean you think she's been biding her time all these years, waiting for the opportunity?”

“I don’t think it could be as calculated as that,” Mallory said. “Remember that she wanted to direct *Macbeth* this summer. If she had, there wouldn’t have been a role in it for Daman. But Sir Iain said no, and suggested *Romeo and Juliet*, and she suddenly saw her chance to hurt both Sir Iain and Daman's father at once.”

“If that’s really what happened,” Bob said. “As Jupiter might put it, we haven’t proved it yet.”

“No, we haven’t!” Califia said emphatically. “Madhuri Singh wasn’t the only Indian girl in Britain!"

Bob had a lot of sympathy for Califia's viewpoint. Clearly Califia thought Madhuri Singh was an excellent director, and she'd had a good experience working with the woman. Bob had seen more than once that if you liked a person, it was a lot harder to imagine they'd done anything bad or wrong.

"Still, let's explore the possibility," Mallory said to Califia. "You told us earlier that Madhuri had counseled you not to fall in love with Daman Duwalia. Can you tell us anything more?"

"Well," Califia said. "She was teasing me, talking about how just because Juliet was in love with Romeo, that didn't mean I needed to be in love with Daman. And she said it was better to avoid a man like him, who might well turn out to be a 'professional lover' as she called him – someone who flirted and seduced and then left you cold. She said she'd met a couple of men like that. Oh my gosh!"

Califia's eyes widened and she put her palm over her mouth.

"What?" Bob asked. "What is it?"

"I just remembered," Califia said. "She told me she'd once been engaged to a man who broke off their engagement – and when it happened she almost killed herself! Of course she was laughing when she told me, and you know how melodramatic she can be. Still, she said that maybe that was why she likes Shake-

220

speare so much − because love and death are intermingled in his plays."

"She used the term 'professional lover'?" Bob asked.

"Yes," Califia said. "I think so."

"Take a look at these," he said as he pulled copies of the threatening anonymous letters Daman Duwalia had received out of his backpack and handed them to Califia. She read them quickly, then handed them to Mallory, who studied them.

"These are really interesting letters," she said in a thoughtful tone. "Even if I didn't already suspect Madhuri Singh of having written them, I would have thought they'd been written by a woman. After all, 'lover' is a word a woman would use more than a man would. It's normally romantic − but in this case, it's sarcastic."

"Or bitter and angry," Bob agreed. "And the writer uses 'lover' in all three notes. 'Lover baby', 'lover parents', and 'Yama the great lover.' What do you think, Califia?"

"Wouldn't a man use the word as quickly as a woman would?" she said.

"Maybe. But not in that way," Mallory said.

Califia looked dismayed, then nodded

her head reluctantly. "You're probably right," she said. "But how are we going to find out if Daman's father and Madhuri Singh actually *were* engaged once?"

There was silence as they considered this question. "I suppose we could just ask Daman to ask his father," Califia suggested.

"What a good idea," Mallory said. "Simple and elegant. Maybe Bob should be the one to call, though."

Bob had tucked his cellphone into the outside pocket of his backpack. He pulled it out, flipped it open, and called Daman. The phone rang six or seven times before he answered. After explaining that Califia had told him Daman's parents' story, Bob said that he was curious to know the name of the woman his father had been engaged to, long ago. Well, more than curious. For reasons he didn't want to explain in detail yet, he really needed to know the answer.

Daman told Bob he was almost certain he could reach his father right away and that he'd call Bob back as soon as he knew the name.

Bob felt a growing sense of excitement. Just last night Jupiter had intimated that perhaps they wouldn't get to the bottom of this case – that it might remain all suspicion and no proof. This might be just the thing to crack the case wide open!

When his phone rang, he took the call immediately, but his heart fell when Daman said that his father couldn't remember the name of the girl his parents had engaged him to. It had been twenty-five years, and he'd said that once he'd married Daman's mother, he hadn't ever thought of the English woman again. Bob thanked him and hung up, shaking his head. He'd thought they were on the verge of a breakthrough, and now this. Pure frustration.

"There has to be a way to find out," Mallory said. "Let me think."

Fifteen minutes later they were going over everything one last time when Bob's phone rang again. It was Daman calling back, and Bob could tell at once that something new had happened. Daman was speaking quickly and quietly and sounded shaken.

"Where are you?" Bob asked.

"On the steps outside the theater. I just had the strangest experience in the hallway," Daman said.

"What happened?" Bob said.

"I don't think I should talk about it on

the phone," Daman said. "I've got a lot of stuff to do, but can you guys meet me tomorrow afternoon? I know you're coming to the dress rehearsal, but this really can't wait. Say, at two? I'll meet you outside."

"Are you all right?" Bob asked. "You don't sound too great."

"I'm O.K.," Daman said. "Not great. I'll see you tomorrow." He hung up, and so did Bob. He looked at Califia and Mallory, wondering what to say.

"What's wrong?" Mallory asked.

"Is Daman all right?" asked Califia, looking very worried.

"I'm sure he is," Bob said. "But something new has happened, and he wants to meet us tomorrow at 2:00. Since I have to work at the library this afternoon, I think I'd better get going. I'm going to need to get in touch with Jupiter and Pete."

He put his laptop, cellphone, and papers back into his backpack, then picked it up and shrugged into it. Mallory walked him to the door and waved, and as he bicycled back to his house, Bob wondered if she might be warming up to the idea of going climbing with him on the cliffs outside Palisade Point. Back at home, he called Pete, then Jupiter, to bring them up to speed.

First he told them about the thank-you note Sir Iain had written to his father, and how it seemed to prove he hadn't written the anonymous letters. Then he told them about Mallory's theory that a woman had probably written them. He also told them Califia's stories about Daman and Madhuri Singh, and Mallory's theory that Madhuri Singh and Daman's father had been engaged once – ending with the fact that Daman had called to say that something new had happened, and that he wanted to tell them about it in person.

Jupiter didn't seem all that surprised by the last bit of information, but Pete was electrified. To be honest, Bob's own head was whirling a bit. Just when he'd imagined they were reaching a conclusion, there was another complication. As he sat at the desk in his bedroom repacking his backpack for the library, Bob suddenly felt worried that writing up this case might prove as hard as solving it to begin with!

12

One Highly Unusual Nut

When the phone rang in the kitchen, Pete was outside with his father, helping him with the deck he was building on the back of the house. Pete loved working with his father; he wasn't generally a big talker, but he was an excellent workman and very good at what he did. Martín Crenshaw hadn't gotten to be the head of set construction for a major studio on his good looks, Pete thought. He was highly skilled, as well as organized and efficient.

He'd taught Pete the value of having all plans made before construction began – though you could do many things by the seat of your pants, building wasn't one of them. He'd also taught Pete the importance of having the right tools in working order and of knowing where they were. Pete had seen the applicability of these principles many times as he'd worked with Jupiter and Bob on Three Investigators cases. As Jupiter had pointed out, minds were tools, also, and keeping track of things in their cases was crucial.

As they'd dug the holes for the deck's

footers, his father had brought Pete up to date on what was happening with the movie he was just finishing. The movie was called *Bear Valley* and Pete was particularly interested because his father had asked him, Jupiter, and Bob to visit the movie set about a month before, and a complicated case had developed. He was glad to hear that shooting would finish soon. That meant his father would be home for a while.

"And what about you?" his father asked. "What have you and your friends been up to? It's hard to imagine you're taking it easy."

"You're right, Dad," Pete said. "I haven't had a chance to tell you. We're working for Daman Duwalia!"

"Really?" his father said. "I heard he was in town. I met him on the set of that 18th-century British Navy movie."

"I know," Pete said, grinning. "And I saw him at a distance! He's starring in *Romeo and Juliet* up at the Theatre Festival. We're all going to watch the dress rehearsal tomorrow night."

His father was surprised. "I wouldn't have thought Duwalia would be acting in something like that."

"I wouldn't, either," Pete said, setting down the shovel he'd been using. "I thought

Shakespeare was just some old English guy who used complicated language and wrote about things I wouldn't care about."

"Even *I* could have told you *that* was wrong!" his father said. "And I suppose that any good-looking young actor might want to play Romeo."

That's when the phone rang. Although the deck that led to the sliding door wasn't finished, enough of it was in place so that Pete could jump up and run across it. He thought he was just doing his father a favor by answering the call, so when he picked up and found Bob on the other end, he was surprised.

And he was alarmed when Bob told him that Daman Duwalia had sounded frightened when he'd asked The Three Investigators to come to the theater early the following day. After watching Madhuri Singh's supposedly lucky dagger drop to the stage, Pete wouldn't have been surprised to hear that the dagger had grown wings and was now flying through the air.

In fact, Pete was so curious about what had happened to Daman that he could hardly focus on the other information Bob gave him. Daman's father had maybe been engaged to Madhuri Singh? How on earth could *that* have happened? Pete wondered. He agreed to meet Bob and the others at the Salvage Yard the next afternoon, then hung up and rejoined his father.

"Something's happened to Daman Duwalia," he said, when he picked up his tools again. Something he doesn't want to talk about on the phone. He wants to see us tomorrow afternoon."

Martín Crenshaw chuckled. "I can think of a lot of things that *I* wouldn't want to talk about except in person," he said. "Or maybe he thinks his phone is being tapped."

"It can't be," Pete said. "He only has a cellphone."

"Well, you'll find out soon enough," his father said. "Now come and hold this timber while I bolt it."

That evening after dinner, Bob called Pete again – this time to tell him that Worthington would be busy the next day and that neither Leif nor Magnus could take them to the theater for their meeting with Daman. So Jupiter had suggested that they get there on their bikes. It wouldn't be hard until the final hill. Pete was still thinking about what his father had said, but when he mentioned phone tapping to Bob, Bob agreed that was impossible.

By the time it was dark, the deck was done, and Pete was so tired from the hard physical work that he slept very well and woke up later than usual. In fact, he felt a little lazy in the morning, and his pressing concern about Daman Duwalia had almost vanished by the time he arrived at the Salvage Yard on his bike and found Bob, Jupiter, and Mallory already there and waiting. Pete wasn't late, exactly, but the others seemed impatient to get going, so Pete didn't really even climb down from his bike. He just turned it around and led the way back out through the gates.

To tell the truth, Pete was glad to be out on a bike with his friends. A lot of the last few days had been spent inside – at the theater and in the car and in typewriter shops – and although yesterday he'd been working outside with his father, today the smells of summer were all around him.

The sun slanted down with its usual intensity, but the air was dry and the clarity of the light made everything vivid – the silver-gray sickle-shaped leaves of the eucalyptus, the German Shepherd barking at them from inside his chain-link enclosure, the turkey buzzard circling overhead. They'd been biking along in single file for a while, but when Jupiter pulled up even with him, Pete was glad to have the opportunity to talk.

"So what do you think?" he asked. "Was Madhuri Singh really engaged to Daman's father?"

"It's an interesting hypothesis," Jupiter said. "But only time will tell."

Pete sighed. Jupiter was fond of saying that, and Pete found it rather frustrating. After all, as far as he knew, time didn't say much of anything.

"What you mean," he said, "is we'll have to wait and see. But you're not very good at waiting."

Jupiter smiled. "No," he said. "I'm not. I'm trying to think of a way we could find out for sure who the girl was, but I'm running into roadblocks."

"At least we know Sir Iain didn't type those anonymous notes," Pete said. "So when are you going to confront Reginald Ward?"

"What are you guys talking about?" Bob yelled from behind, where he was riding next to Mallory.

Jupiter turned around as he was riding. "Nothing the two of you don't already know," he said.

They were reaching the eastern outskirts

of Rocky Beach now, and traffic was sparse. There were times when all four of them could ride abreast, but mostly they stayed in pairs. Pete didn't like it when a car came up fast and leaned on its horn. The houses out here were on larger parcels of land, and they passed an occasional fenced field of dried bleached grass where a horse was quartered.

The elevation rose as they got closer to the mountains and soon they were on the long approach to the theater. Pete rose out of the saddle and rode standing up, putting maximum pressure on each pedal as it climbed to the top of its arc. He saw he was outdistancing the others, but he didn't care. It was good for him, he thought. He needed the workout.

He got to the top first, and was standing, panting, drinking from his water bottle as the others straggled in. "Come on, you guys," Pete said. "We've got to get you in shape!"

They were all catching their breath when Daman Duwalia appeared.

"Wow!" Pete said. "How did you know we'd gotten here?"

"I've been watching for you," Daman said. "I told Bob I'd meet you outside."

He pointed to a wooden bench in the shade of a large live oak. "Let's talk there."

Mallory, Daman, and Jupiter sat on the bench, and Bob and Pete sat on the grass in front of them. Despite the beautiful day, the warm soft wind and the smell of the grass under the oak, Daman's face looked pinched and his lips were pressed together.

"Thanks for coming," he said. "I'm probably just being paranoid, with everything that's been going on. But yesterday something happened after Bob called me about my father that I really can't explain."

"What was it?" asked Pete.

"I hope it wasn't another falling dagger," Mallory said.

"Or a magnetized one," Bob said.

"Let's let Daman tell us what it was," Jupiter said.

"Well, after Bob called me and I talked to my father and then called Bob back, I was walking down the hall to get something from one of the vending machines when I ran into Madhuri," Daman said. "She was standing in the hall talking to Cory Johnson. You remember him – the electrician guy?"

"Yes," Jupiter said. "I met him last summer at the Salvage Yard."

"When the two of them saw me, they both looked startled, and Madhuri fell over herself being super-friendly. It was really odd."

"Have you ever seen them together before?" Mallory asked.

"Sure," Daman said. "Lots of times during rehearsal she or Billy would give Cory instructions about one thing or another. But I'd never seen them talking outside the theater. Anyway, it was none of my business why they were talking, but Madhuri went into overdrive to explain to me that there'd been a brief power outage on the set, and that she was worried it might affect the dress rehearsal."

"Had you noticed a power outage?" Bob asked.

"No," Daman said. "But Madhuri said it was only on the set. Anyway, Cory looked confused, as though he'd never even heard of a power outage. He said — really clearly and really loud — 'I thought you wanted to talk about this thing with Daman's father.'"

"'This thing with Daman's father'," Jupiter repeated, picking some grass apart with his fingers.

"*What* thing with Daman's father?" Pete asked.

"I think that's what's worrying Daman," Mallory said. "That he'd just talked to his father on the phone, and now here was Cory

Johnson referring to him. How did Madhuri Singh react?"

"She looked like she wanted to kill him," Daman said. "That was really what made me paranoid − or at least suspicious. She started talking really fast − babbling sort of, like she was trying to find the right words − until finally she said that the intercom must be broken and that Cory had misunderstood.

"Cory said, 'What did I misunderstand?' and she said 'I didn't say '*Daman's father*', I said, 'A *layman* wouldn't *bother*.' She went on to say that most people wouldn't be worried about a minor power outage but, as a professional, it was her responsibility to make sure there was no problem."

Jupiter pinched his bottom lip.

"Clever," he said. "She was counting on similar-sounding words to misdirect you. The woman can think on her feet."

"She certainly can," Daman said. "But there's no way Cory could ever be an actor. He was so confused I felt sorry for him. He just started stuttering and waving his hands around. He's not very good with people in general, but this was really extreme."

"I know what you mean," Jupiter said. "When he was buying lighting fixtures at the

Salvage Yard last year, he had real trouble making eye contact, and he didn't seem to know how or when to say simple things like 'please' and 'thank you.' After he wrote the check and left, Aunt Mathilda raised her eyebrows at me and then took her finger and twirled it around her ear in a circle."

Pete started laughing. He could just see Aunt Mathilda doing that — even if it wasn't terribly polite!

Daman cracked a half smile at Pete's laughter. "But that isn't all," he said. "Suddenly Madhuri's hands were on Cory's shoulders and she was turning him around and sending him off with a little shove, telling him to check every electrical circuit on the stage. After he wandered off shaking his head, she turned to me and said out of the blue what a good actor my father is — how she'd never met him, of course, but she'd seen a number of his movies. The thing is, she's never mentioned my father before."

"Curiouser and curiouser," Jupiter said.

"So as I said, maybe I'm just being paranoid," Daman said. "But since I'd just been talking to my father on the phone, it seemed almost as though Madhuri must have heard me."

At this point, Daman stopped talking and looked directly at Bob.

"You didn't tell me why you wanted me to ask my father what the name of the woman he'd been engaged to in England had been, but after that scene in the hallway, I could guess. You think it was Madhuri, right?"

Bob nodded. "Well, really, it was Mallory who thought that."

"It seems weirdly possible," Daman said. "But what I really can't imagine is how Madhuri could have overheard my conversation when the door to my dressing room was shut."

"My father said maybe your phone line was being tapped," Pete said.

"I actually thought that, too," Daman said, "until I realized there's no easy way to tap a cellphone."

"No," said Jupiter thoughtfully, "but there's a very easy way to overhear a conversation in a room. All you have to do is bug it."

"Bug it!" Pete almost yelled. "Of course! I should have thought of that! Let's go search for the bug!"

"Agreed," Jupiter said. "But before we do, I have a confession to make. I've been an idiot about Cory Johnson. When I was on my back on the catwalk, staring up at the lights, it should have occurred to me that Cory Johnson is an electrical engineer. He may well have put in those lights, and he certainly could have installed an electromagnet under a steel rim. In fact, he's exactly the sort of person who would be an excellent technical accomplice."

"That's true," Mallory said. "We agreed that neither Sir Iain nor Madhuri Singh had the know-how to pull all this off, but Cory Johnson does. A lot better than Reginald Ward ever would. On top of that, he was in the control room the night of the technical rehearsal. He could have controlled the switch that turned the electromagnet off and let the dagger fall."

"So someone else," Jupiter said, "with a much wider vision and a much more complicated plan came up with all the separate ideas, and then, one at a time, Cory Johnson executed them."

"That's quite a word to use when you're talking about the dagger," Daman said.

Jupiter smiled. "Let me rephrase. 'And then Cory Johnson did as he was told. As in *Star Trek: The Next Generation,* when Jean-Luc Picard intones, 'Make it so,' and the crew scampers to do his bidding."

Pete thought that was pretty funny. He didn't know Jupiter had ever seen *Star Trek.*

"And Cory, of course, would have figured out how to pipe those infrasonic sounds into the theater and even into Daman's dressing room," Bob said. "Maybe we should just confront him."

"Not yet," Jupiter said. "It's all conjecture at the moment − all *could be* rather than *is*."

"The only problem with the theory," Mallory said, "is that if we're having trouble pinning down a motive for Sir Iain, Madhuri Singh, or Reginald Ward, Cory Johnson would seem to have no motive whatsoever."

"I don't see that as a problem," Jupiter said. "The only motivation Cory Johnson needs is to please whoever it is he's working for. We just don't know who that is yet."

"I'm still holding out in favor of Madhuri Singh," Mallory said.

"Let's go look for the bug!" said Pete. "We don't have all day. We have to go home and have dinner and get dressed and get back here in time for the rehearsal tonight."

"That's right," Jupiter said. "I have a mind to put Pete Crenshaw in charge of time management for The Three Investigators."

Since the theater was air-conditioned, it was a lot cooler inside, and although Pete generally preferred being outside to being inside, the chill felt good. They paused before the door to Daman's dressing room, and Jupiter whispered.

"Perhaps this goes without saying," he said, "but once we're inside, no one should say anything. If the room is really bugged, then anything we say inside could be picked up."

"Right," Pete said. "Let's go." He couldn't wait to get inside and tear the place apart. Well, not tear it apart, exactly, but give it a good going over. If there was a listening device of some sort, he'd find it. At least in the movies, they were little tiny black things that transmitted any noise. Informants wore them under their shirts when they went to get some criminal to confess, and F.B.I. guys were fond of hiding them on lamps. That's where Pete would look first.

"O.K.," Jupiter whispered. "Mallory, you take the dressing table and the other furniture. Bob, check the floor, particularly around the baseboards. Pete and I will concentrate on the walls and ceiling."

"I'm also going to check the lamps," whispered Pete. Jupiter opened the door and the other four followed him in. Daman sat in the chair in front of his dressing table while the others went to work. Mallory was carefully pulling out drawers and examining things, while Bob crawled around checking the baseboards. Pete had checked all the lamps and found nothing. One by one they turned and shook their heads in exasperation. Jupiter wasn't having any luck either. Hands at his sides, he was studying the walls.

Pete was beginning to feel that maybe a bug wasn't the explanation, after all, when he began studying the contents of a small shelf. There was a framed picture of a young man and woman in exotic and colorful costumes that Pete supposed must be Daman's parents. He picked it up and looked at it long and hard, but when it revealed nothing, he set it down again, and picked up the plaster statue of Ganesha, the elephant-headed god.

It was fun to have an excuse to look at it carefully – at its in-turned ears, its sleepy expression, its curled trunk, its basket full of nuts – and as Pete tilted it, something rattled and he was suddenly filled with adrenaline. He tilted it again, and it rattled again. Looking closely, he saw something on top of the nuts in the basket. It wasn't black as he'd supposed, but camouflaged to look like one of the nuts. He had to keep himself from shouting in triumph. He'd found the bug! He held it up and smiled with glee, while the others crowded around him, and Mallory clapped him on the shoulder and said, "Great going, Pete!"

13

A Very Useful Phone Plan

Fifteen minutes later, as Mallory, Pete, Jupiter, and Bob bicycled back to the heart of Rocky Beach, the bug was in Jupiter's pocket. When Mallory had suggested simply crushing it, Jupiter had said he wanted to preserve it as evidence – but he had wrapped it in a handkerchief and assured her that small bugs like this one only worked a short distance from their electronic source.

Mallory was actually glad it hadn't been crushed, since when Pete had found it, she'd been genuinely thrilled. She had thought Madhuri Singh was the villain for a long time, and now she was certain. After all, according to Daman himself, Madhuri had put the murtis in Daman's dressing room to begin with – ostensibly to welcome a fellow Hindu.

Ha! Mallory thought. Madhuri's plan had been in place almost from the start. Maybe Cory had installed the listening device after he'd switched the threatening murtis for the benevolent ones. When he'd put back the thoughtful and amused Ganesha, he'd made sure it had come with his own personal bug, so Madhuri could keep track of how well her plan was progressing.

Before they'd started biking away from the theater, Mallory and the others had talked about what they'd discovered. Madhuri had been the one who heard Daman talking to his father, but Cory Johnson had allowed her to do that by planting the bug. All the confusion, all the multiple suspects faded away, and Mallory had been pleased that at last Jupiter and the others were convinced of what she had intuited almost from the start. The evidence against Madhuri Singh might be circumstantial, but there was a lot of it.

Even so, Jupiter had made it clear he didn't want to confront Madhuri on the circumstantial evidence alone. As he had pointed out, if even part of the web of clues was incorrect, the whole case collapsed.

As Mallory bicycled along, she reflected that apparently Madhuri hadn't been bothered when Daman had called in The Three Investigators. She had underestimated their capabilities and thought they would simply fall at once for the trail she'd laid from the anonymous letters to the typewriter in Sir Iain's office. Only when she overheard Daman asking his father the name of the girl in England to whom he had once been engaged did she start to panic – or at least to realize that The Three Investigators were cleverer than she'd assumed.

Of course, in this case, it was *she*, Mallory, who had been clever. She had seen almost at once that there was a strong possibility that the girl in England might have been Madhuri Singh – though, to be fair, she thought that Bob, too, had seen the possible connection pretty quickly. She was bicycling beside him, but he and Jupiter and Pete were all silent on the ride.

Mallory suspected that was because they really thought it would be impossible to prove that Madhuri Singh had once been abandoned by Daman's father. She smiled to herself. She thought she'd finally devised a way to prove it, but she didn't want to share it with The Three Investigators until after she knew whether her plan had worked.

After all, even though she'd been truly helpful with two of their past three cases, the first time had been an accident of sorts, and the second time she'd just done what they'd asked her to do – although she'd done it well.

This was different. This was something she'd thought of doing on her own, and if it worked, it would prove that her hypothesis about Madhuri's motive had been correct. In fact, this was her big chance – her chance to prove to Jupiter, once and for all, that she could be an asset, not a hindrance, in future investigations. As she bicycled along, she did some calculations in her head.

It was already late afternoon, and Mallory would be seeing Pete, Bob, and Jupiter again in just a few hours. Bob's mother and father were taking the three boys to the dress rehearsal and Mallory's mother was taking her. Mallory understood that a lot of people had been invited to come tonight – that the theater was going to be almost full of community members like Bob's parents – so she broke the silence of the bike ride to ask Bob to save her a seat in case she was a little late.

"Why would you be late?" Bob asked.

"I've got something to do when I get home," she said. "It's about the case, but I don't want to talk about it until I see whether or not it works."

"O.K." Bob said. "I'll make sure there's an empty seat next to us."

A little while later, when Mallory and the others came to the outskirts of Rocky Beach, Mallory waved goodbye to the boys and headed toward the Wessex House. There, she had dinner with her mother, then took a shower and dressed for the theater – though the whole time she was eating and getting ready, she was examining her plan from every angle to see if it had any flaws.

When her mother had had a landline installed in the apartment, she'd chosen a calling plan that let them call sixty countries – so that they could call Scotland without worrying about the cost – and after she'd gotten home, she'd researched the phone company's international calling plans. Soon she found herself staring at a list of sixty countries from Australia to Zimbabwe.

There, in the middle, between Iceland and Ireland, was India. Mallory smiled with satisfaction. Jupiter wanted hard evidence? Mallory had a plan to supply him with that.

When she'd spent the morning in the library with Bob, she'd made special note of the newspaper article Bob had sent to her about Sir Iain Anthony having been knighted. The reporter had gone to Stratford-on-Avon to interview people who had known Sir Iain at the theater there, and one of them had been Madhuri's father Arjun Singh. Was he a talker! Now that his daughter had moved to America, he said, he and his wife hoped to return to his family home in Jaipur in the Indian state of Rajasthan as soon as he retired. He said he had moved to London as a young man, where he had become an accountant and had met his wife. He had gone on at length about the theater in Stratford-on-Avon and about Sir Iain. He was a reporter's dream.

That day, Mallory had wondered if indeed Mr. Singh and his wife had retired to India, and though it had taken her a long time and many false starts, she thought she had tracked him down. She had a street address and a telephone number for Mr. Arjun Singh, Jaipur, Rajasthan, India. If she could talk to him — pretending to be someone other than Mallory MacLeod, and calling for a different reason altogether — she might be able to get the confirmation she needed.

"Mallory," her mother called. "Are you ready? We have to leave soon if we don't want to miss the first act."

Mallory opened the door to her room and stuck her head out. Her mother was sitting on the couch in the living room. "I have to make a phone call," Mallory said. "I'll just be a minute."

She shut the door. She didn't want to

make them late, of course; but even more, she wanted to find out what she could, and even though she'd be calling a city where it was twelve and a half hours later than it was in Rocky Beach, she'd wanted to wait as long as possible before calling. By now, it was finally early morning in Jaipur – but hopefully not so early that someone shouldn't be up in the Singh household.

Earlier that summer, on The Three Investigators' second case, Mallory had also pretended to be someone she wasn't in order to convince a corrupt professor to give her a copy of a letter he had forged. Maybe she wasn't as good an actress as Califia, but Mallory thought she'd done a pretty good job.

Tonight she planned to be Maisie Campbell – down from Edinburgh for the summer to do an internship at *The Telegraph* in London. She was writing an article for *The Scotsman*, back home, on the custom of arranged marriages among British Indians. Her Scottish accent would come in very handy, she thought.

Mallory had her notes in front of her as she picked up the receiver and stared at it for a moment. She knew that you could block the location of the call you were making by dialing *67, and she obviously didn't want Mr. Singh to know that she was in California, not in London. She wasn't sure if blocking the location worked between countries, but she had to give it a try.

Mallory was feeling a bit nervous – or maybe not nervous, but excited. Or maybe not excited, but scared. Whatever the name of it was, she was feeling something. She dialed *67, then 91 – the country code for India – and then the number. She heard clicking and buzzes, and then the digital tones that let her know that the number was being dialed. Just when she expected the phone to start ringing, she got a series of high-toned beeps – two beeps and a one-second silence followed by two more beeps. She listened in disbelief. The number was busy.

Of all the things she'd expected – that this was the wrong Arjun Singh, that Arjun Singh wasn't there – the line being busy had not been one of them. She hung up and stared at the phone. She could almost hear her mother in the living room getting more and more restless. Mallory waited as long as she could stand to and then dialed the number again.

This time the phone started to ring – not a ring like you heard in the States, but a ratcheting sort of noise, like a stick being dragged on a washboard. With each ring, Mallory's heart beat harder. The phone rang three times, and then someone picked up.

"Namaste," a male voice said. "Yah Arjun Singh hai."

"Mr. Singh?" Mallory said. "My name is Maisie Campbell, and I'm from Edinburgh. In Scotland."

"Edinburgh?" Arjun Singh said. "This is a surprise. Do I know anybody in Edinburgh?"

He had switched seamlessly to English, which he spoke with a lovely lilting accent. His voice modulated musically throughout his sentences and tended to rise at the end.

Mallory laughed lightly. "Well, you don't know *me*, Mr. Singh. I'm actually calling from London. I'm interning at *The Telegraph* for the summer, and I've been assigned an article about arranged marriages among British Indians."

"If I may ask you," Arjun Singh asked, "how did you come upon my name?"

"I was doing research for another earlier article, about Sir Iain Anthony, and I found an interview you gave about working at the theater in Stratford-on-Avon. You seemed so articulate and forthcoming that I thought you'd be a natural interview subject."

"Oh, Sir Iain!" Mr. Singh said. "Such a nice man. Well, I am sure there are many Indians you could have asked in London, but I am flattered you took the trouble. How may I help you, young lady?"

So far, so good, Mallory thought. She'd found the right Arjun Singh.

"I was hoping you could help me write a first-rate article by sharing your experiences with the marriage you arranged for your daughter Madhuri."

Mr. Singh was silent for a moment, and Mallory was afraid she'd trodden on territory that he found too personal. "It was a sad disappointment," he finally said. But then his voice got cheery again. "Maybe better to say that it didn't work out as her mother and I had hoped it would."

"I'm sorry to hear that," Mallory said, "but before you go on, I just wanted to assure you that I won't be using any real names in the article, so you should know that your privacy and your daughter's privacy will be protected."

"That is most kind of you," he said, "but it is many years ago now, and though it was very difficult at the time, I'm sure that everyone has put it well behind them."

"I'm very glad to hear that," Mallory said. If Madhuri's father only knew! she thought. "Did you know the boy's family?"

"Oh, no," he said. "It was arranged through a matchmaker, like so many arranged marriages. Well, there are many ways, of course, but that is the way we chose. You see, I was homesick and wanted to come back here to Jaipur after I stopped working, so we asked the matchmaker to find Madhuri a husband back home in India."

"How did you go about that?" Mallory asked.

"We met with her and we talked about the sort of son-in-law we were looking for. We wanted her to marry a Hindu, of course, and someone whose family was as well off as ours. And she used Madhuri's horoscope. She found a number of suitable matches, but the family that seemed best to us was the Duwalia family."

There was knocking on her bedroom door. Mallory hurriedly put her hand over the receiver.

"Mallory?" her mother called. "We're going to be late."

She calmed herself as best she could and said as levelly as possible, "Just a minute,

Mom. I'll get off the phone as soon as I can."

"Oh, Mallory!" her mother said, but she didn't open the door.

She took her hand away. "I'm sorry, Mr. Singh. What were you saying?"

"Only that perhaps it was for the best. When the marriage was first arranged, we had no idea that Madhuri's future husband was going to become an actor. Some people think that is not very reputable."

"When did you first meet the matchmaker?" Mallory asked.

"Oh, we consulted with her when Madhuri was just thirteen, and by the time she was fourteen or so, the marriage had been arranged. She and the Duwalia boy were supposed to get married after Madhuri turned 18, right after secondary school. There is a child marriage law saying the boy must be 21 and the girl 18, but we were not too worried about the boy."

"And if I may ask," Mallory said. "What happened?"

"Madhuri was always very obedient, but some Indian children are not. She allowed herself to dream of the wedding back in India, of the party we would have, of her life as the wife of a good husband. She wrote the boy letters and sent him pictures. This was before e-mail, of course, and all that video chatting they do, so it took a long time for packages to go back and forth. She had her heart set on it." He sighed. "But the boy fell in love with someone else and wrote to tell Madhuri he wouldn't marry her. This was even before he had settled the matter with his parents! A headstrong boy!"

"And your daughter – ?" Mallory asked.

"She did not take it very well at all," her father said, "and I was very angry with the Duwalia boy. My mother and I were frightened Madhuri might harm herself."

"But she didn't," Mallory said.

"No," Arjun Singh said, "and I give thanks for that. But it changed her life – maybe even for the better. She decided to move to California – to go to school there in order to start over. She has been very successful in America."

"I'm glad to hear that," Mallory said. "If I could switch subjects for a minute – . In the interview you gave about Sir Iain Anthony, you said that Madhuri was very impressed with him."

"Oh, yes," Mr. Singh said jovially. "She had a big schoolgirl crush. Though I have often wondered if taking her to see *Macbeth* at such an early age was a bad idea. Those witches! And the play is so violent. Macbeth and his wife had a terrible marriage and set such a bad example!" He chuckled lightly.

"Madhuri has never married, and I have sometimes wondered if, between *Macbeth* and the Duwalia boy, she has soured on the whole idea. Of course, after seeing *Macbeth*, Madhuri wanted to be an actress herself. She practiced around the house, and I thought she was very good! But a teacher told her she had no talent and she became very discouraged."

This time, Mallory smiled − eight thousand miles away from Madhuri Singh's father in Jaipur. If only he knew, she thought, just how good an actress his daughter had become!

"Well, I hope she's happy now," Mallory said.

"Oh, yes," Mr. Singh said proudly. "She is a big success, as I said, but she says she is happy at home, as well. She is dating an electrician! No actors! She had a crush on Sir Iain and then almost married a man who became a Bollywood star, and now she has someone with a good solid profession − almost as solid as accounting. From what I understand, he also knows a very large amount about computers."

"I'm glad to hear she's happy," Mallory

said.

"Mallory!" her mother called sharply.

"Thank you so much, Mr. Singh," she said. "You have no idea how helpful you've been."

"Well, I am glad, Ms. Campbell," Mr. Singh said. "It has been a pleasure to speak with you."

After Mallory hung up, she sat for a moment in the afterglow of her triumph. She'd done it. She was bursting with happiness at the thought that she could give Jupiter, Pete, and Bob what they needed to confront Madhuri Singh and Cory Johnson and wrap up this bedeviling case. And she hadn't even done anything dangerous!

Nessie – the long-necked replica of the Loch Ness monster she'd won earlier that summer at a Scottish music camp – looked up at Mallory from her pride of place on the immigrant's trunk The Three Investigators had given her. Mallory picked her up and kissed her on the nose, then put her carefully back where she had been, patted her own name – painted on the front of the trunk – and raced out to join her mother.

It was clear to Mallory that her mother was annoyed with her, but she didn't say anything on the way to the theater – although when they got there, the play was already well underway. There *was* a large audience attending for free on the night of the dress rehearsal, and Mallory's mother found a seat on an aisle toward the back. Mallory waited until her eyes adjusted to the darkness, then spotted The Three Investigators just six rows from the stage, and she hurried down to join them.

The boys whispered hello, but they were clearly engrossed in the play, and now wasn't the time to tell them what she had just done. Mallory tried to focus, but the details of her conversation with Arjun Singh kept playing over and over in her mind. She found she was able to pay attention during the fight scenes – the semi-comic scene between Tybalt and Mercutio, which ended when their play fighting turned tragic and Mercutio was accidentally killed. The scene swiftly followed in which Romeo, in a rage, went after Tybalt and killed him.

Mallory was impressed with the fury Daman communicated, as well as with his sword fighting skill. Though she knew that the fight had been very carefully choreographed, it looked utterly spontaneous. She was surprised to see that the parrying dagger Daman held in his left hand looked a bit like Madhuri's good luck charm, not like the daggers she'd seen in the prop room. It must be a trick of the light, Mallory thought, since the dagger that had fallen from the sky was locked securely in Sir Iain's office.

Mallory's attention wandered again until Califia's big scene – the final scene of the play. Romeo staggered in to Juliet's family tomb where Juliet's body lay, distraught at the news that Juliet had killed herself and unaware that it was all a ruse and that soon she would awaken. Califia lay motionless on top of the catafalque as Daman took the apothecary's poison and swiftly died. Califia came awake from her drug-induced slumber not long after. There was Friar Lawrence, come to see if his plan had worked and finding devastation instead. Frightened by noises outside the tomb, he tried to get Juliet to leave with him, but she would not.

Alone in the tomb, Califia looked radiant in her grief. She kissed Daman's lips, hoping some drop of poison remained. When nothing happened, she knelt on the slab on which she'd previously lain and grabbed Romeo's dagger from its scabbard. "O happy dagger!" she cried. "This is thy sheath!"

Something flickered on Califia's face, so

briefly Mallory wondered if she alone had seen it, and then, rather than facing the audience, arching her back, and plunging the dagger into her chest – as she had when Mallory had seen the scene before – Califia turned away from the audience, to obscure the sight of her stabbing herself in the heart.

The play ended, as it always did, with a short scene in which Romeo's and Juliet's parents reckoned with the result of their long and bitter feud, and the Prince of Verona told the assembled crowd: "Go hence, to have more talk of these sad things/ Some shall be pardon'd, and some punished/ For never was a story of more woe/ Than this of Juliet and her Romeo."

When the curtain fell, the theater was filled with applause and shouts of approval. The curtain rose again, and the cast members took their bows, but Mallory saw that, far from looking triumphant and happy, Califia looked unnerved.

Mallory would find out why later on, she thought; right now, she had to tell The Three Investigators about her call to India. As Jupiter, Pete, and Bob stopped clapping, Mallory said, "Listen, you've just got to hear this," then told them as quickly and concisely as she could about her conversation with Arjun Singh.

"Wow!" Pete said. "You really talked to him in India?"

"That's incredible," Bob said. "I'm floored. That shows − well − ingenuity, courage, and determination. And other stuff!"

"I couldn't agree more," Jupiter said. "And Arjun Singh was absolutely clear that his daughter and Daman's father were engaged to be married?" he added.

"Not only that," Mallory said triumphantly, "but he told me she was in a romantic relationship with an electrician. So now we know why Cory is cooperating with her. Her father also told me she had wanted to be an actress once."

"And boy," Pete said, "she would have made a good one!"

"Yes," Jupiter said, "she's fooled a lot of people. Including me."

But not me, Mallory thought happily.

"The only thing I still don't know is what Sir Iain has to do with all of this," she said. "But right now we ought to go backstage and congratulate Califia and Daman."

"Yes," Jupiter said. "After that, we can decide how to move forward with our information."

The wings were crowded with actors and well-wishers, all of them in a jubilant mood. With Mallory leading, the four of them threaded their way through the crowd until Mallory spotted Califia sitting on an upturned wooden box backstage. Daman was sitting next to her.

When she saw them, Mallory was startled; she'd have thought the two leads would be in the thick of it, accepting their admirers' congratulations. She wanted to ask Califia why she'd changed the way she played the final scene, but now was clearly not the time. Califia looked shaken to the core.

When Califia saw Mallory and the boys, she got to her feet. "Oh, Mallory!" she said and gave her a long hard hug. When Mallory hugged her back, she could sense that Califia almost didn't want to let go.

"Califia!" she said. "What's the matter? You were terrific. It's going to be a smash."

"Yes," Bob said. "We should all be cheering."

"You won't believe what happened," Daman said. "I feel terrible."

"What did you do?" Mallory asked him.

"He didn't do anything," Califia said. "You probably didn't even notice but the last scene didn't exactly go according to plan."

"I did notice," Mallory said. "I was going to ask you."

"Everything was fine," Califia said, "until I pulled the dagger out of Romeo's belt. It didn't feel right, not like the collapsible dagger I've been using – it felt heavier, and different, and when I lifted it up in the air, the lights caught the blade and I could see that patterning you were talking about."

"Damascene?" Mallory asked.

"Yes," said Califia. "I could see Damascene patterning on the blade and I realized that the lucky dagger that was supposed to be locked in Sir Iain's safe was somehow in my hands, and I was about to plunge it into my chest!"

Mallory was stunned, and she saw that the boys were as well. "So that's why you played the scene differently!" she said.

"Yes," Califia said. "My first impulse was to drop the dagger or scream or something, but then I was afraid I'd ruin the whole entire play. So I turned to the side and thrust the dagger between my left arm and my ribcage, hoping the audience would believe what they couldn't really see."

"I'm so proud of her," Daman said.

"She carried it off and stayed totally in character. Amazing."

"Yes, but look," Califia said. "I cut my dress." She showed them the spot where the dagger had slashed the fabric.

"Who would do a thing like that?" Daman said. "I should have noticed the dagger wasn't the right one. I use it to parry Tybalt's rapier in the scene where I kill him. I put it back in its scabbard, as I was supposed to, before the fatal rapier thrust, but I didn't notice a thing, I had so much adrenaline coursing through my veins."

"This is very worrying," Jupiter said. It seems to complicate something Mallory found out tonight that I thought had brought us to the end of our path and which I'm sure will be of great interest to both of you. But right now I have only one thought. Where's the dagger now?"

"I kicked it under the catafalque as I died," Califia said. "It should still be there. They haven't touched the set. What I want to know is how it got out of that locked safe!"

"Come on," Mallory said, "before the crew starts taking things apart."

She led the way toward the raised block of wood painted to look like granite.

14

A Devious Scheme

Jupiter followed Mallory out onto the stage. The spots had been turned off, and high above, on the ceiling, the can lights he'd stared at the other day shone dimly. Jupiter was feeling a lot of admiration for Mallory and Califia – Califia for her quick thinking and courage and Mallory for her inspired action in finding and calling Arjun Singh. But what he was feeling even more strongly at the moment was incredulity at how he had missed something staring him straight in the face until just five or six hours before.

He'd even met Cory Johnson the previous summer, and though he'd noticed that Cory wasn't very good with people, Jupiter had been in no doubt about how proficient he was with both the practical side of inventing and the theoretical side of electrical science. He had talked Jupiter's ear off, and Jupiter had been able to follow little of it. Yet not once since the case had begun – not even after running into Cory in the prop room and learning that he was still working for the theater – had Jupiter considered Cory a suspect until after Daman had told his story about how Cory had acted in the hall.

The thing that amazed him most of all was that he hadn't thought of Cory even *after* he had come to his conclusions about the electromagnet and the infrasonic rumblings. And how had he not paid attention when Sir Iain had reassured Madhuri about his safe's electromagnetic lock? Sir Iain might as well have said he was leaving the safe wide open.

Pete and Daman were down on their knees peering under the catafalque.

"It's under there," Pete said. "I can see it, but I can't stick my hand in far enough."

Daman was still in costume. "Will this help?" he asked. He took off his rapier and handed it to Pete.

"Perfect!" Pete said. On his stomach, Pete jiggled the rapier under the catafalque, and after a few swipes, he managed to catch the dagger and it came scooting out. He scrambled to his feet as Califia picked it up and stared at it as though somehow *it* – and not the person who'd placed it in the scabbard on Daman's belt – had been responsible. She handed it to Pete for safekeeping – a good choice, since Pete was certainly better than any electromagnetic lock.

As Bob, Mallory, and Califia crowded around Pete, talking and staring at the dagger, Jupiter pinched his bottom lip. Enough self-recrimination, he thought. Now was the time to apply his mental faculties. By finding out for certain about Daman's father and Madhuri – and especially by finding out about Madhuri and Cory – Mallory had almost closed the case. But she was still puzzled by what Sir Iain Anthony had to do with everything, and Jupiter had finally formed a working hypothesis on that. If his guess was right, it had been Sir Iain all along who Madhuri Singh was after, and not Daman at all. Daman had been a bonus – two birds with one stone – and also useful as a way to cast further doubt on Sir Iain.

No, Madhuri had been hurt and angry when the position she had wanted – the theater's artistic directorship – had gone to Sir Iain the summer before. She would have been hurt and angry if anyone other than she had gotten it, but there must be something in her past – something connected to Sir Iain himself – that had made it far worse. Jupiter did not yet know what it was, but he intended to find out.

Whatever it was, it had almost certainly been exacerbated by Sir Iain's refusal to let her direct *Macbeth*. As it turned out, despite her breezy affect, she was very ambitious, and Sir Iain had seemed like an easy enough target – an old white man with Parkinson's. She had wanted to push him out.

If she could cast doubt on Sir Iain's competence, if she could make people think that one of the results of his Parkinson's was a steadily worsening dementia – it was, after all, Jupiter had discovered, one of Parkinson's possible complications – if, in the words of Worthington's correspondents, she could make people believe Sir Iain was "losing his marbles," then everything became simple. The board of directors would apply pressure, Sir Iain would resign, and there she would be, ready and available to take his place.

There would be no need to prove anything in particular – why peoples' skin crawled and their stomachs knotted when Sir Iain spoke in public; why malevolent representations of Indian gods had shown up in Daman's (and supposedly Madhuri's) dressing rooms; why threatening anonymous letters had been typed on the typewriter in Sir Iain's office; how a fire had started in his wastebasket and could have burned the theater to the ground; how a dagger he supposedly had under lock and key had magically appeared in the hands of the lead actress in the play about to open, a dagger that could have killed her, a dagger that had magically fallen from the sky, almost killing – but not really – the director of the play.

All of this came together with the rumors Madhuri was helping to spread and that were raging through the theater's community like one of California's wildfires – poor Sir Iain, poor demented Sir Iain, once a great actor, but now out of his mind, waging an obscure vendetta against two Indian Hindus.

All of it had been carefully calculated and fiendishly clever. What a terrible, devious scheme, Jupiter thought. But the source of Madhuri's rage at Sir Iain Anthony – that was still a mystery. Perhaps the very last thing that had happened – Califia finding the dagger in her hands – had been an accident, Jupiter thought, a mix-up in the prop room, maybe. From what he'd been able to ascertain, Madhuri had warm feelings for Califia, so why would she want to hurt her? It wouldn't further her plot very much.

Madhuri had personal reasons for resenting both Sir Iain and Daman. Because the attacks on Daman mirrored the supposed attacks on her, she'd managed to divert attention from herself even as she got back at both men at once. But she had no reason that Jupiter could see to target Califia.

It was time to act, Jupiter thought, and the course of action was clear.

"If I may have your attention," he said, and his friends all stopped talking and turned to him. "I think the time has come to talk to Sir Iain." The others all agreed.

With Jupiter leading, and Pete carrying the dagger as though it needed constant attention, the six of them walked through the wings, out the stage door, and down the hallway until they reached Sir Iain's office. Jupiter was happy to see that he was there, sitting in his desk chair under blazing lights, and looking delighted to see them. When Jupiter knocked on his door, he peered through the glass wall of his office and jumped to his feet.

"Come in, come in," he said, ushering them into his office.

"Daman, Califia," he said. "You were magnificent. This will be such a success." He smiled with pleasure and turned to Jupiter, Pete, Bob and Mallory.

"I don't believe we've met," he said to Mallory. "I'm Iain Anthony."

Mallory smiled. "I think everyone knows

who you are, Sir Iain," she said. "I'm very pleased to meet you. I'm Mallory MacLeod, and these are my friends."

"Welcome, Miss MacLeod," Sir Iain said. He shook her hand warmly before turning away and seeing what Pete was holding. Pete held the dagger before him, cradling it in his hands, and a look of puzzlement and disbelief crossed Sir Iain's face.

"But that's in my safe," he said. "Or are there two of them?"

"That's why we've come to talk to you, Sir Iain," Jupiter said. "The lock to your safe was disabled and the dagger retrieved. It's all part of a clever plot we wanted to share with you."

"A plot?" Sir Iain said.

"Yes, indeed," Jupiter said. "A plot to push you out of your position as artistic director of the theater. Pete, would you be so good as to give Sir Iain the dagger?"

Pete proffered it to Sir Iain who took it as if it were poisonous. He looked quite concerned as he went back around his desk and sat down in the chair, putting the dagger on the desk before him.

"Please," he said. "I know I don't have seating for this many, but make yourselves as comfortable as possible. Now tell me what you've discovered."

"It's been very confusing," Jupiter said, "with lots of misdirection, but we've finally seen our way through to an understanding. It's our belief that Madhuri Singh – out of anger and frustration that you got the directorship instead of her, and for other obscure reasons that I'm sure will come to light – has been working quite relentlessly to discredit you, to cast doubt on your ability to do your job, and to suggest to the people at the theater and the community at large that you are not fit for the job."

Jupiter was impressed with Sir Iain's reaction. He did not jump to believe what Jupiter had told him, nor did he rush to contradict it. He looked neither pained nor pleased, just interested, as though the person being discussed as the victim of a plot was someone other than himself.

"I'm sure you have proof," Sir Iain said, "or you wouldn't have come to me."

"We don't have proof, exactly, but we have a compelling story with only one possible conclusion," Jupiter said. "Let me start at the beginning. I'm afraid it goes back to the opening Gala. Were you aware of any negative reactions to the speech you made that night?"

Sir Iain's eyebrows rose and fell and a smile crossed his lips. "Yes," he said, with a humorous tone. "I heard that some patrons thought I should have made a career not of Shakespeare but of *The Creature from the Black Lagoon*." Everyone laughed. Sir Iain's voice was rich, strong and melodious, Jupiter thought.

Jupiter carefully lined up the points in his mind before he began. "We believe, Sir Iain, that your microphone was tampered with, that the lighting on you was subtly altered to make you appear frightening, and that sounds below the human range of hearing were piped into the theater, making people feel apprehensive and afraid."

Jupiter turned to Daman and asked him to tell Sir Iain what had happened when he'd begun rehearsals − before he'd contacted The Three Investigators − and Daman explained about the feeling of fear he'd felt when the murtis were switched, and about the anonymous letters he'd received; he went on to tell Sir Iain about the listening device Pete had found in the basket of nuts held by Ganesha.

Jupiter filled in the rest, explaining that Mallory had discovered that Madhuri and Cory Johnson were romantic partners as well as partners in crime, and that he had no doubt that Cory's technical expertise had resulted in the subsonic sounds, the dagger falling from the sky, and the failure of Sir Iain's electromagnetic lock.

This last, Jupiter told Sir Iain, had had a particularly dangerous result. In the final scene of the play, when Califia had grabbed Daman's dagger, she'd discovered she was holding not the collapsible prop dagger she was used to but Madhuri Singh's 'lucky' dagger. Had she not had her wits about her, she might have badly injured herself or even stabbed herself to death, he said.

At this, Sir Iain looked absolutely stricken. Up until then, he'd been reacting to the details of a plot directed against him with total aplomb, but the fact that Califia had been in danger cut him to the quick.

"But you're quite all right, my dear?" he asked solicitously.

"Yes, Sir Iain," Califia said. "Still a bit shaky, but all right. I wish the same could be said for my dress." She showed Sir Iain the slash she'd made in the fabric when she brought the dagger down.

He stood now, and he looked to Jupiter like a man much younger than he was − resolute, determined, strong, and capable.

"I must tell you," he said, "how extraordinarily impressed I am that you managed to see to the bottom of this. It's a tangle that would have caused fits for Agatha Christie herself!"

"Unfortunately," Jupiter said, "as I mentioned when I began, it will be difficult if not impossible to prove all this. I'm sure that Cory Johnson used a computer to aid him in his various tasks, and an examination of the computer system might indeed yield forensic evidence. But then again it might not."

Sir Iain rocked back in his chair for a moment, tented his hands, and thought.

"What you say is undoubtedly true," he said, "but I think there may be an easier way to get at the truth. Because Madhuri Singh, no matter what she has done, is not all bad, you see. She is a gifted director and a very smart woman, and she has a good heart, I think.

"A good heart!" Pete said. "Well, maybe. But she has a bad personality!"

"A bad character, too," said Mallory.

"I suggest we summon her to the office, right now, and see if she will admit what she's done," Sir Iain said. "As you may be aware, I have a bit of experience with acting, and perhaps if I play my role well, I can get her to confess. I have no doubt that the story you're telling me is correct — too much of it makes perfect sense and answers questions I've long had — but Madhuri, at least so far, has not truly hurt anyone, at least not physically, and while we could involve the police — ."

"We know Chief Reynolds!" Pete said.

" — I don't see the point of it," Sir Iain finished. "The poor woman must feel tortured to have gone to these extremes, and that torture is punishment enough. Of course, I'll fire her and Cory at once — ."

"Oh, no!" Califia cried.

" — and take over as the director of *Romeo and Juliet.*"

Califia looked relieved.

"But I've known for a long time now — and partly from playing them onstage — that villains are quite ordinary human beings who most often think that the actions they take, which others find so objectionable, are really quite reasonable."

Sir Iain paused and looked around the room.

"Also, I have lived long enough to know that most people have, at least once in their lives, felt envy or jealousy or hurt feelings so intense that they did dangerous or damaging things. I know I have. But they do not then go on to make a career of that. No, I think that letting Madhuri and Cory go will be punishment enough. As for Cory, I feel rather sorry for him. I imagine that he never quite grasped the scope of what Madhuri was attempting and was merely doing whatever his partner asked him to do."

The wisdom and humanity of Sir Iain's speech moved Jupiter greatly, and he made a note to remember this moment forever. Sir Iain had been maligned, slandered, and greatly wronged, and yet he had quickly found the grace and forbearance to forgive Madhuri Singh.

"I must say," Sir Iain concluded. "I wish I could remember meeting Madhuri in Stratford, but it is so many years ago now I have no memory of it at all. She was a young girl, and so it makes sense that she would remember meeting an older man. But I do remember her father – Arjun Singh, in the payroll office – now that you remind me of him."

"Now," he said. He opened the top drawer of his desk, swept the dagger into it, and closed it gently.

He sat forward and pressed the button on the intercom on his desk. "Madhuri, can you hear me? It's Iain."

Jupiter was shocked to hear the name Iain, with no "Sir" attached. He'd gotten so accustomed to "Sir Iain," he'd begun to think that was the man's name. The intercom squawked and screeched, and then Madhuri Singh's voice came through. "Yes?" she said.

"Could you come to my office for a moment, my dear?" he said.

"On my way," Madhuri said.

Sir Iain smiled warmly at all of them. "I'll do the talking," he said. "No need to feel anxious or uncomfortable. Relax as much as you can. And enjoy the show!"

That made Jupiter laugh.

When Madhuri Singh appeared in Sir Iain's door, she looked startled to see that the room was full of people. "Come in, Madhuri," Sir Ian said. "Always room for one more. I was just congratulating our principals, and I think you've met their friends?"

"Yes," Madhuri said, quite graciously, it seemed to Jupiter under the circumstances.

"I wanted to tell you," Sir Iain said, "what a fine job you've done with the production. The rehearsal tonight was splendid, and I'm sure that tomorrow night's opening will exceed everyone's expectations. So bravo!"

Madhuri glowed in the warmth of Sir Iain's praise.

"I also wanted to say how very much I admire you. Not everyone would have been able to overcome their disappointment and spin it into gold as you have."

"I – I'm not sure I understand, Sir Iain," Madhuri said.

"Naturally you were disappointed when I was given the artistic directorship over you. Who wouldn't have been? But a lesser person might have brooded about it or let it get to her. Instead, you're back this summer and doing a wonderful job."

Sir Iain was the model of magnanimity and sincerity, Jupiter thought. He could make a stone weep. His voice was a rare instrument and he spoke the lines he had chosen for himself with a largeness of spirit that was quite inspiring. He was mesmerizing, even hypnotizing. What an actor! Anyone would believe anything he said.

The effect his words had on Madhuri Singh was already apparent, Jupiter could see. She knew she was not really the person he was praising, and her shoulders fell a little and her face became tense.

"Nevertheless," Sir Iain went on, "these

young people have just told me the strangest story, and I felt I should ask you directly. They suggested to me that you were trying to make it seem as though I were losing my mind so that you could assume the position after all. Preposterous, I know, and I don't believe a word of it, but I called you here to see if you could help solve what seems to me a very great mystery."

Calmly he opened his desk drawer and pulled out the dagger.

"Does this look familiar to you?" he asked.

Madhuri was shocked. "Why – why yes," she said. "It looks like the dagger that fell from the ceiling during the tech rehearsal – the one we put in your safe to keep it secure."

"So why do I have it here?"

Madhuri Singh was trying to think as fast as she could, Jupiter saw.

"Perhaps," she said, "because you took it out of the safe?"

"But that does not explain how it wound up in Califia's hands during the play's climactic scene," Sir Iain said, "and how it thus came very close to killing not Juliet, but Califia." He turned to her. "My dear, would you please show Madhuri the slash you made in your dress when you chose to thrust the dagger between your ribcage and your arm rather than into your heart?"

Califia stood up and stretched the dress to show the slit. Under the slash, her skin was visible.

Madhuri gasped and her hands flew to her cheeks. "Oh, my God," she said, her voice filled with horror. "That was never supposed to happen! I told Cory not to do that! No one was supposed to get hurt!" She took a step toward Califia and reached out to her. "Oh, Califia," she said. "Thank God you're all right."

"So perhaps you do know, after all, how the dagger escaped from my safe?" Sir Iain asked. The look on his face was complicated, Jupiter thought − triumph at having played his part so well and sympathy at how easily Madhuri had given herself away − and all because she cared about Califia.

Madhuri opened her mouth to explain, or defend herself, or deflect, but no words came out, and she seemed on the verge of tears − though Jupiter could tell it was not grief she was feeling but something closer to anger and frustration. She stopped herself, took a deep breath, and − to her great credit, Jupiter thought − began defending Cory.

"It wasn't Cory's fault," she said. "He did what he did because he loves me, and he just doesn't know when to stop. He gets confused, sometimes, about what's real and what's not. He's played far too many video games and the line between what's permissible online and in real life gets blurred for him sometimes."

"I'm not sure we understand," Jupiter said. "I think we'd all like to believe you, but you're going to have to explain more clearly before we do."

Madhuri looked at him as if seeing him for the first time. Jupiter realized that even though she had known, through bugging Daman's dressing room, that he was the head of an investigative firm Daman had brought in to discover who was writing him anonymous letters, she had never accurately gauged the danger he presented to her plans.

Madhuri looked deflated and defeated. "I mean that Cory unlocked the safe and put the dagger in Daman's scabbard. Daman was supposed to use the dagger in the fight scenes, but then realize what it was and lose his concentration – lose his cool on stage. The whole thing was a plot to rattle Daman. I knew the choreography of the fight scenes. I knew the dagger wasn't used to hurt anyone. And because Sir Iain had put the dagger in his safe, we thought suspicion would fall on him."

She turned to Sir Iain. "On you, Sir Iain, for being so careless. You couldn't be trusted. That, together with everything else and you'd have to resign."

"Oh, my dear," Sir Iain said. "I'm so sorry."

"But Daman never even noticed the dagger had been switched," Madhuri said in frustration, "and when Cory suggested that we should put it back in Daman's scabbard for the final scene, I told him absolutely not. He thought it would ruin Califia's focus, but I said under no conditions. After Charlotte Mitchell put the collapsible dagger in Romeo's scabbard, Cory must have replaced it. Oh, I wish I'd never seen that dagger. Keep it away from me! Please, throw it out!"

Her face was deeply flushed and she was breathing hard. Jupiter could see that she was passionate, and often had acted in the grip of deep feelings. Perhaps such feelings were necessary for success in the theater.

Personally, he thought that calm detachment had its bonuses when it came to the fields of detection and investigation.

15

A Dramaturgical Dagger

Two days later, in his bedroom, Bob carefully packed his backpack with all the climbing gear Coach Fogerty had issued to him – the long thick rope, two harnesses, the helmet, the chalk bag, the assortment of chocks and pitons – and also the climbing shoes he'd bought, as well as a lunch he'd made for two.

He'd invited Mallory to go climbing with him, and she had said she would. Though Bob was by nature a cautious person, generally more comfortable with things he already knew or understood, he thought the time had come for that to change. He admired Pete, who took on the world full-throttle even though he was at times nervous and even frightened.

Bob wanted to be more like that. He had a tendency to hold back, to play it safe, to assess the risks and possibilities before acting. Sometimes, he saw, it was beneficial to jump into things without thinking about them too much. It was time to take some risks.

Of course, he'd already taken some this summer – first in starting to write up The

Three Investigators' cases and post them on-line, and then in showing Mallory that he liked her. In fact, those risks had actually paved the way for going climbing with her. He slipped his backpack over his shoulders, and fifteen minutes later he was pedaling into the Salvage Yard.

He enjoyed the debriefing he and Pete and Jupiter had at the end of each mystery – a debriefing in which they tied up loose ends and made sure everyone knew everything that had happened. It was a great help to him when he wrote up their cases. And besides, it gave him a real feeling of pride to think back over what they'd accomplished. Today, he was also hoping Pete and Jupe might help him with the title for the new case. He'd thought of several possibilities and he wanted to pick the strongest one.

Pete and Jupiter were nowhere to be seen, but he found them inside Headquarters, where Pete was smiling and Jupiter looked unusually happy, too. Bob's gaze fell to the desk in front of Jupiter. Madhuri's Singh's "good luck" dagger lay there, its leather sheath beside it.

"Wow!" Bob said. "What's that doing here?"

"Sir Iain came by the Salvage Yard this morning," Jupiter said. "Charlotte Mitchell drove him. I happened to be in the office with Aunt Mathilda. You could have knocked her over with a feather when she saw Sir Iain."

"I wish I'd been here!" Bob said.

Pete, who'd been trying hard to keep silent, erupted.

"I got here about two minutes beforehand, so I saw everything," he said. "Charlotte drove Sir Iain's silver BMW, and when he climbed out, he said to me and Jupe, 'Gentlemen! So good of you to receive me!' Pete repeated these words in a terrible English accent.

"Then Aunt Mathilda came out on the office porch and threw her hands in the air," he continued. "'Land sakes!' she said. 'What a beautiful car! And do my eyes deceive me or is that Sir Iain Anthony? My word. You were so wonderful as the evil king in *The Dark Castle!*'"

Bob laughed at how vividly Pete remembered exactly what Aunt Mathilda had said and what a good job he did of mimicking her.

"Sir Iain smiled and kissed Aunt Mathilda's hand when I introduced her to him and to Charlotte," Jupiter said. "I thought she was going to swoon. Then she said, 'Well, don't let me keep you. I'm sure you have important business to attend to!' She hurried back onto the porch and disappeared. I don't think I've ever seen Aunt Mathilda act bashful before," he added.

Bob didn't think he had, either. "But what did Sir Iain say?" he asked curiously. "And why did he give us the dagger?"

"Charlotte had told him we collected mementos from our cases, and he thought the dagger should be our memento for this one," Jupiter said. "Madhuri had claimed she never wanted to see it again, and Charlotte found the scabbard in the control room at the back of the theater where Cory worked. Sir Iain wanted to bring them in person to thank us for our help."

"Actually, he said 'invaluable assistance,'" Pete said. "He also told us he hoped that when we saw the dagger we'd remember him and what he called 'the little adventure we shared.' I said he could bet on that! I'll never forget that dagger dropping from out of nowhere. We can hang it next to the California Cornucopia poster Mallory gave us."

Pete picked up the dagger, slipped it carefully into its sheath, snapped the leather guard shut, then walked to the wall and held it up.

"How does it look?" he asked Bob and Jupiter.

"Good," said Bob.

"Impressive," said Jupiter.

"Fantastic!" Pete said.

After Pete set the dagger back on the desk, Jupiter explained to Bob that Sir Iain had also come to explain what had happened since the three of them had last been at the theater.

In the first place, Sir Iain *had* let both Madhuri Singh and Cory Johnson go and had taken over as director of *Romeo and Juliet.*

"From what he told us," Jupiter said, "opening night went very well, and the run is almost sold out. He also reported that he'd been bothered by Madhuri Singh's animosity, and suspected it was more complicated than her disappointment at not being offered the job he'd gotten. That kind of bitterness and resentment seemed unnatural, he thought, unless it had causes rooted in the past. So he was curious."

Bob listened intently as Jupiter explained that Sir Iain had taken the admirably direct route of asking Madhuri Singh about the time they had met – so many years before at the theater in Stratford-on-Avon – and why, when they'd begun working together in Rocky

Beach, she'd pretended she'd never met him.

"And she told him?" Bob asked.

"In detail," Pete said. "I suppose she was glad to get it off her chest."

Jupiter went on to explain that Madhuri had been eleven years old when her father had taken her to see Iain Anthony starring in *Macbeth*. She'd been enthralled by the whole performance, but especially by Sir Iain. When her father saw how impressed she was, he'd asked her if she'd like to meet the man − convinced that because he worked at the theater he could get his daughter backstage that very night.

"Sir Iain doesn't remember any of this," Pete interjected. "It was so long ago, and she was just a kid."

"It's true, I think," said Jupiter, "that events like this impress themselves on children far more than they do on adults."

It seemed that Arjun Singh had succeeded in getting his daughter backstage, where Iain had been friendly and gracious, according to Madhuri Singh's own account. Sir Iain had been about to leave for his dressing room when Madhuri realized that she hadn't brought her autograph book. After all, she hadn't known she'd need it, and she became very upset at the thought that she'd missed her chance.

"Sir Iain told her not to worry," Pete said. "He invited her to come back after any performance and told her he'd sign her autograph book right in his dressing room."

"The invitation thrilled her," Jupiter said. "Not just meeting the actor and talking with him. Not just getting his autograph. But meeting him in his dressing room."

"I get that," Bob said. "Like she'd been invited to a secret special place that very few people got to see. So what happened? I guess the bad part's coming up."

Bob had guessed right. Jupiter went on to explain that several days later, Madhuri had tried to get backstage with her autograph book. But she'd been blocked by a rude and nasty stagehand who'd told her she had no business bothering the actors. When she explained that she'd been invited, he shook his head in disgust and told her to get out of there. When she persisted, he yelled at her and pushed her rudely, making some nasty remark.

"She fell and skidded on the wooden floor, and a long splinter went into her knee," Jupiter said. "Her mother tried to get it out with tweezers, but it broke."

"Ouch!" Bob said.

"Yeah," Pete said. "Really painful. The part her mother couldn't get out stayed in her knee for a long time until it finally dissolved. She was just a kid, and she blamed the whole thing on Sir Iain."

"So all these years, she's been nurturing a grudge?" Bob asked. "That's pretty scary."

"It gets worse," Jupiter said. He told Bob that, in spite of what had happened with the stagehand and the splinter, seeing *Macbeth* had ignited in Madhuri a love affair with the theater. In fact, for a long time she'd wanted to be an actress, just as her father had told Mallory. After her junior year in high school, she'd applied for a summer internship at the Stratford theater. Unfortunately, she'd been roughly rejected by an administrator who told her she had no talent whatsoever.

By that time, Iain Anthony had become quite famous, and it seemed that Madhuri couldn't open a newspaper or magazine without reading about him. Sir Iain had told Pete and Jupiter that as the years went by, and he became more famous and received various awards and was in the public eye, she resented him more and more.

"He told us he thought he must have become a constant irritant, like the splinter she

291

couldn't remove," Jupiter said. "She came to the United States to get away from all that, and of course to get away from what had happened with Daman's father. She was still so young, and so many things had gone wrong. I feel genuinely sorry for her."

Bob did, too. Even before Jupiter's re-telling of what had happened in the past, he'd had the suspicion that Madhuri Singh wasn't malicious — just a person being driven by forces she herself didn't understand. She'd gotten wrapped up in the intricacy of her own plot, and when she'd done the bad things she'd done, she'd been able to rationalize them.

"She was a really unhappy person," Pete added. "She thought she'd been rejected un-fairly both by Daman's father and by the man at the theater, and she felt bitter and angry. But she knew that if she behaved the way she felt, she wouldn't get anywhere."

"So she started behaving like the Mad-huri Singh all of us met," Jupiter said. "Calm, professional, in control. She started de-ceiving everyone around her — lying to them in little ways and big ways. Sir Iain thinks it must have given her a lot of pleasure to see how good she'd gotten at lying — how she fooled everyone. If only that guy at the theater who'd said she had no talent could see her now, she thought!"

And all that time, Bob thought, she'd never gotten over her delusion that it was somehow all Sir Iain's fault, and when she lost the artistic directorship to him, it had just proved too much. She'd concocted her plan and put it into action. Bob shook his head when he thought of how close she'd come to succeeding.

"Here's the part I think will appeal to you the most, as a reader and a writer," Jupiter added. "After Madhuri told him what had happened, Sir Iain concluded that the splinter that had gone into her knee at the theater – long and thin, sharp and painful – got lodged in her imagination and years later was transformed into a dagger. He said the human mind is a very curious thing, and that Shakespeare himself might have seen Madhuri's story as rich fodder for a dramatic tale."

Bob was amazed at the magic of this. Sir Iain's insight thrilled him. In fact, the great Shakespearian actor had intuited something that had been a mystery to Bob. What had the dagger been doing in this story to begin with? The switched murtis were intended to make it seem that there was a vendetta against Hindus, and the anonymous notes were meant to do the same.

But the dagger had never been meant to kill or harm anyone − though it would have done a better job than any of the blunted prop weapons. Its fall from the sky had been orchestrated to look as though it had been intended for Madhuri, and to a child of eleven, it might well have seemed as though the splinter that entered her knee was a dagger aimed at her very heart.

"Wow!" Bob said. "That *does* appeal to me. A lot. And, naturally, since I'm thinking ahead to writing up this case and this is our fourth case this summer, I'm glad the word 'dagger' starts with the letter 'd'! Still, I could use your help deciding what the adjective should be. I have three possibilities, but I haven't decided which is the best."

"What are they?" Pete asked. "I bet 'dangerous' isn't one of them. Not fancy enough."

Bob nodded. "It isn't. My mother lent me a book at the beginning of the case called *Darwin's Moral Mammals,* so the word 'Darwinian' has been on my mind. A dagger is double-bladed, and so are a lot of emotions − like ambition and deceptiveness −

that the human species evolved to have."

"Interesting," Jupiter said.

"And then there's Damascene," Bob said. "For a while I thought I might be able to use that, but even though it's the pattern on the dagger's blade, it can also be used to describe an instantaneous conversion. But so far all the titles have been metaphors that related to what happened in the case, and that one wouldn't be."

"And number three?" Jupiter asked.

"Dramaturgical," Bob said. "Madhuri talked about actions we take being dramaturgical when they're aimed at achieving a particular purpose. I'm still thinking about that one. I'll let you know as soon as I've figured it out."

It had suddenly occurred to him that in a little while he'd be with Mallory, and that he might want to put off a final decision until after he'd also talked with her. She'd be great at discussions like this one.

Just then the phone in Headquarters rang. Jupiter hit the speakerphone button.

"Three Investigators Headquarters," Jupiter said. "Jupiter Jones speaking."

"Oh, great, you're there!" a now-familiar voice said. "It's Daman Duwalia, Jupiter. I'm calling to thank you again, and to tell you how well opening night went. Califia was terrific, and Sir Iain picked up the director's duties as though he'd held them from the beginning. Everything went off without a hitch. I think it's going to be a success."

"From what I've heard, it certainly will be," Jupiter said.

"Anyway," Daman went on, "although I understand why you might not want to see *Romeo and Juliet* again, I'm calling to let you know that the next time I'm in a movie that premieres in L.A., I want to invite you all to the opening. I'll send tickets, and you can come with me to the party afterwards. It'll be a lot of fun."

"I can hardly wait!" Pete exclaimed. "Will it be another *Time Twist* sequel?"

Daman chuckled. "I don't know, Pete. Maybe."

After they all thanked him and Jupiter hung up, Bob looked at his watch and saw that it was time to go. Mallory and her mother were supposed to pick him up in front of the Salvage Yard's office in about ten minutes and he didn't want to be late.

"Have fun," Pete said, "and be careful!"

As he left Headquarters, Bob felt remarkably good. He was glad that the dagger had wound up in their possession, and the details he'd gotten from Pete and Jupiter about Madhuri's story filled in the blanks in his notes.

Mrs. MacLeod was right on time, and they were in Palisade Point before noon. The popular climbing routes were on a series of cliffs near the sea, and part of a state park. Mrs. MacLeod dropped them off. She had some errands to run and would be back in three or four hours. Bob and Mallory surveyed the rock wall they hoped to climb, then settled down at a picnic table to eat the lunch Bob had brought.

Mallory unpacked the first sandwich. "Tomato, lettuce, and cheese!" she said. "This is great. By the way, I ran into Skinny yesterday. He and Reginald Ward aren't 'bros' any more. Or at least Reginald Ward isn't friends with *him*. I guess he wanted Skinny to frighten Jupiter, and when that didn't work the way he hoped it would, he dropped Skinny. They weren't really friends to begin with. After all, as we said, poor Skinny doesn't have any friends."

"Poor Skinny," Bob said. "Have you decided whether to call him Egret or Elm?"

Mallory laughed. She shook her head. "You almost have to feel sorry for the guy."

"Almost," Bob said. But then he thought that he was being too harsh, and in future he ought to give Skinny a break. If this case had taught him anything, it was that sometimes people became who they were for reasons that weren't immediately apparent. Maybe Skinny just couldn't help himself.

Nah, Bob thought. Skinny was just a jerk, and he worked hard at it.

As they ate, Bob brought up his quandary over the titles, explaining to Mallory what he'd talked about with Jupiter and Pete.

"What do you think?" he asked.

"All three are unusual words, of course," Mallory said. "But before I give you my opinion, you'd better explain your thinking."

"I've already pretty much decided against 'Damascene,'" Bob said. "I've been going with titles that are metaphors that relate to what happened in the case, and although 'Damascene Dagger' might be a metaphor for *something*, I don't think it would have much to do with what happened with Madhuri Singh."

Bob stopped and unwrapped a second sandwich. "I like 'Darwinian Dagger' much better because, as my mother would say, none of us are born as blank slates. We're preloaded with impulses and instincts, and Madhuri Singh was being driven by a bunch of them at once. Ambition and deceptiveness were both at the heart of this case, and Madhuri Singh took both of them too far."

"That's true," Mallory said, helping herself to a second sandwich. "And I see what you mean. Ambition like Sir Iain's can result in great achievements and a glorious career, but when it gets twisted, as it did with Madhuri, it can lead to ruin."

Bob smiled. Mallory was great at this. It wasn't that Pete and Jupiter wouldn't have gotten it, but it would have taken longer and wouldn't have been as satisfying.

"That's right," he said. "The weird thing is, deceptiveness is not only a necessary tool for survival but it can also be a necessary tool for getting at the truth. When you deceived Arjun Singh and Jupiter deceived that guy at the typewriter shop, you both used the capacity to deceive for a good purpose, but when Madhuri Singh cooked up her plan to blacken Sir Iain's name and reputation, she used the same capacity for a bad one."

"So what about 'dramaturgical'?" Mallory asked. "That one you're going to have to explain."

"O.K.," Bob said. "Here goes. Do you

remember the first time we ever saw Daman and Califia together on stage, the afternoon they rehearsed the final scene?"

"Sure," Mallory said. "That's what let me know something was wrong the night of the dress rehearsal."

"Remember before they ran the scene, Madhuri Singh was talking about the word 'dramaturgy' as it's used in sociology?" Bob asked. "She was saying that all of us, all the time, play roles – that we essentially go through life acting?"

Mallory nodded. She finished her second sandwich and Bob pulled out the peaches and oatmeal raisin cookies he'd brought for dessert. He took out his pocket knife and cut the peaches into quarters.

"I've thought about it a lot since then," Bob said, "and I'm convinced it's true. When I'm at school or with my parents, I'm different from the way I am when I'm with Jupe or Pete – or you."

"But is that really acting?" Mallory asked.

"In a way, I think it is," said Bob. "And in the case of Madhuri, she played a role for so long that she got lost in it. Only the shock of realizing that Califia could have been seriously hurt made her stop acting, all of a sudden. So that's why I'm thinking of calling the case *The Mystery of the Dramaturgical Dagger.*"

"I see what you mean," Mallory said. "That even though we all need to play roles, it can be dangerous if you let it get to a point where you lose track of who you really are. You've got to be open to other people and take risks with new situations."

"That's just what I was thinking earlier about taking risks," Bob said. "It's true about a lot of things – even climbing. I've never told you this, but when I was younger, I broke my leg when I was climbing alone. So I wanted to risk climbing again. And this is going to be the first time I've ever done roped climbing. I hope I can figure out how to do it!"

He took a deep breath. "So, what do you think? About the titles?"

Mallory thought for a moment. "To be honest, I like both of them," she said. "As long as you pick the right details to include, I don't think you could go wrong with either one of them."

"That's what I was afraid you'd say!" Bob said, mock-groaning.

They finished their lunch and took their gear over to the rock face where they'd begin their climb. As the more experienced climber, Mallory would lead the first pitch. They'd both rope up and Bob would start to belay her, but she'd have to climb to a place where she could put an anchor in and clip the rope through it before his belaying would really work. After she started to put in anchors, if she misjudged her feet and slipped, she wouldn't fall far because Bob would be able to arrest the fall by holding the rope tight.

As she fastened her harness and helmet – both of which she'd brought with her – Mallory smiled at Bob and he smiled back. He liked her a lot. Of course, he understood by now that he liked her more than she liked him – at least in that particular way – but even so, he had a feeling that she saw being with him as something that made her more herself.

He stood at the base of the cliff as she started to ascend, keeping a close eye on her progress, but also thinking that although it had been fun to talk to first Pete and Jupiter and then to Mallory about possible titles, in the end he'd have to follow his own instincts and choose the title he thought best. Pete, Jupiter, and Mallory were entitled to their opinions, naturally, but in the end, writing wasn't a democratic process. The final decision lay with the writer. And in this case – and all of The Three Investigators cases – that writer would be Bob Andrews. Him.

As for the title, there was a lot to be said for 'Dramaturgical.' Jupiter had been right when he'd guessed that the part of the case that would appeal to Bob the most was Sir Iain's insight that after the splinter had gone into Madhuri Singh's knee, it had lodged in her imagination for good, and years and years later had transformed itself into a dagger. So *that* was settled, Bob thought.

Up above him on the cliff face, Mallory had started to put in chocks, attaching carabiners through which to thread the rope he held. She was literally in his hands now; she was trusting him with her life.

That was what human beings needed to do, Bob realized – to trust instead of mistrust, as they made their way through life. Still, people were awfully slippery. They lied all the time, for both good reasons and bad ones – and as it turned out, lying was not only an essential survival tool, but also led to one of the best things about human existence – the ability of people to tell and appreciate fictional tales.

In fact, a lot of the instincts human beings were born with – including lying – cut two ways, Bob thought. Human instincts had evolved through a process of trial and error, and in the world as described by Charles Darwin, human beings had the power to choose their own paths in life – though the right path and the wrong path could lie as close together as the twin blades of a dagger.

Above him, Mallory had completed the first pitch. She'd stopped climbing and wrapped the rope around her back. Her voice sounded surprisingly distant when she called out "On belay!" to let Bob know she was ready for him to start. Bob lifted the leg he had once broken in three places, set the tip of his toe on a narrow rock projection, reached up with his right hand, grabbed an equally narrow handhold, and started to make his way up the cliff.

ABOUT THE AUTHORS

Elizabeth Arthur

Elizabeth was born on November 15, 1953 in New York City. She is the daughter of Robert Arthur, the creator of The Three Investigators series. She was educated at Concord Academy in Concord, Massachusetts, the University of Michigan in Ann Arbor, Michigan, Notre Dame University of Nelson, British Columbia, and the University of Victoria in Victoria, British Columbia.

Before she started working on the New Three Investigators series in December of 2018, Elizabeth spent most of her life writing for adults. *Island Sojourn* – a memoir about building a house on a wilderness island in northern Canada – was published in 1980 by Harper and Row. A second memoir, *Looking For The Klondike Stone,* was published by Knopf in 1992. She is also the author of the novels *Beyond the Mountain, Bad Guys, Binding Spell, Antarctic Navigation,* and *Bring Deeps.*

Elizabeth's writing has received fellowships, grants, and awards from the Bread Loaf Writer's Conference, the Ossabaw Island Project, the Vermont Council on the Arts, and the

Indiana Arts Commission. She twice received fellowships from the National Endowment for the Arts and was the first novelist ever given an Antarctic Artists and Writers Operational Support Grant from the National Science Foundation.

Her novel *Antarctic Navigation* was chosen by the New York *Times* as a Notable Book, received a Critics' Choice Award from the San Francisco *Review of Books*, and was chosen as a Best Book of 1995 by *A Common Reader*. In 1996 the novel received the Ohioana Book Award for Fiction from the Ohioana Library Association.

Elizabeth has also taught creative writing at Miami University in Oxford, Ohio; the University of Cincinnati; and Indiana University/Purdue University of Indianapolis, where she directed the creative writing program. She and Steven Bauer met in 1980 at the Bread Loaf Writer's Conference and have been married since June of 1982.

Steven Bauer

Steven was born on September 10, 1948 in Newark, New Jersey. He was educated at Hanover Park High School in East Hanover, New Jersey, Trinity College in Hartford, Connecticut, and the University of Massachusetts in Amherst, Massachusetts. In 1970 he received a B.A. with Honors in English from Trinity, and in 1975 he received an M.F.A. in English from the University of Massachusetts.

Steven is the author of three books for young people – *Satyrday*, 1980; *The Strange and Wonderful Tale of Robert McDoodle*, 1999; and *A Cat of a Different Color*, 2000. His book of poems *Daylight Savings* was published by Gibbs Smith in 1989 and won the Peregrine Smith Poetry Prize.

Steven's work has received fellowships from the Bread Loaf Writer's Conference and the Fine Arts Work Center in Provincetown, Massachusetts. In addition, he has been given grants and awards from the American Library Association, the Parents' Choice Foundation, the Ossabaw Island Project, the Massachusetts Arts Council, and the Indiana Arts Commission.

From 1979 to 1982, Steven taught literature and creative writing at Colby College in Waterville, Maine. From 1982 to 2009 he taught at Miami University in Oxford, Ohio where he directed the graduate and undergraduate creative writing programs. In 2010 he established Hollow Tree Literary Services, an independent editing business.